EVIDENCE

of Things

NOT SEEN

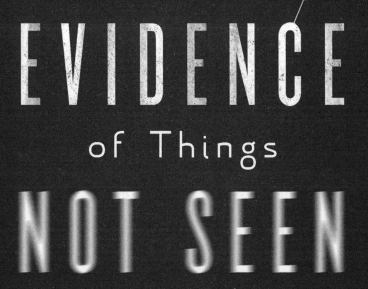

EVIDENCE of Things NOT SEEN

LINDSEY LANE

FARRAR STRAUS GIROUX
NEW YORK

Farrar Straus Giroux Books for Young Readers
175 Fifth Avenue, New York 10010

macteenbooks.com

Library of Congress Cataloging-in-Publication Data
Lane, Lindsey.
    Evidence of things not seen / Lindsey Lane. — First edition.
        pages cm
    Summary: When Tommy Smyth, a high school junior and particle physics genius,
goes missing, multiple lives intersect—or don't—as the residents of a small Texas town
relate, in their separate voices, what each thinks might have happened to Tommy.
    ISBN 978-0-374-30060-9 (hardback)
    ISBN 978-0-374-30063-0 (e-book)
    [1. Missing children—Fiction.   2. Interpersonal relations—Fiction.
3. Genius—Fiction.   4. Country life—Texas—Fiction.   5. Texas—Fiction.
6. Mystery and detective stories.]   I. Title.

PZ7.L2502Evi 2014
[Fic]—dc23
                                                                                2014013167

Farrar Straus Giroux Books for Young Readers may be purchased for business or
promotional use. For information on bulk purchases please contact Macmillan
Corporate and Premium Sales Department at (800) 221-7945 x5442 or by email at
specialmarkets@macmillan.com.

For Gabriella, for always

CONTENTS

KIMMIE JO...................................3

THE PROPOSAL...........................10

ALVIN...34

THE COMIC BOOK......................43

JAMES..54

THE SMYTHES...........................60

HYPOTHESIS..............................70

RACHEL.....................................86

MR. McCLOUD............................95

LOST..103

MARY LOUISE...........................122

WATERMELONS........................129

TIM...147

RITUAL.....................................156

THE LAST DANCE.....................173

NANDO.....................................187

CHRISTMAS ORNAMENTS.........193

HALLIE......................................212

CHUY..219

We leave pieces of ourselves everywhere. Every time we meet someone, they take some of us and we take some of them. That's how it is. Little particles stick us together. Bit by bit. I think it's how we get whole.

—On a piece of notebook paper
found on the side of US 281

EVIDENCE

of Things

NOT SEEN

KIMMIE JO

REALLY? I MIGHT BE THE LAST PERSON WHO SAW
Tommy Smythe?

I didn't hardly even see him, Sheriff. It was Friday afternoon. I was heading back to Fred. You know, Fred Johnson High, because of the Cinco de Mayo dress rehearsal. I had to—um, I had to go home right after school because, well, it was that time of the month and I had to change—anyway, I was driving back to Fred and I saw Tommy coming toward me on that red motorbike of his. Ruby. I heard he calls it Ruby. Isn't that the weirdest? I mean, I named my dolls but that was like in kindergarten. Is that something boys do in high school—name their vehicles?

No, he didn't look any different, Sheriff. He was wearing his lab goggles, so he looked like this nerd scientist on a scooter. But that was how he always looked. Tall, skinny, kind of goofy looking. He would have been cute if he tried a little. He only had acne on his forehead but that's because his hair always hung in front of his face. If you want good skin, you have to take care of it. You know, wash your face and drink a lot of water. For being such a science nerd, you'd think he'd understand that stuff.

I'm sorry, Sheriff. Tommy was driving away from school. I was going toward school. It was a little ways down the road from here. I hadn't passed the entrance to the Stillwell Ranch yet. I'd just gone by this place. You know, the pull-out. I really wish people would call it something else. Like the dirt patch. That's all it is. Do you know that guys at Fred joke about girls putting out at the pull-out and not pulling out at the pull-out? So gross.

Oh, yeah, Tommy. He was coming toward me on his motorbike. It was ten to four. I know because I looked at my watch and knew I'd probably be fifteen minutes late to the dress rehearsal even though I was already speeding. Oops, I probably shouldn't say that to you. Ms. Flores, the ballet folklórico teacher, knew I might be a little late and she was cool with it. I knew my part cold. We were doing a couple of traditional Mexican dances in the center of town on Saturday for Cinco de Mayo. Most people don't believe I'm Mexican until I tell them my whole name: Kimberly Josefina Garcia. That's where Kimmie Jo comes from. Josefina. I look like my dad but with my mom's German coloring.

Did I wave to Tommy? No way. I mean, we're both juniors but we're really different. Like on two different planets. No, we're farther apart than that. He's like a gas molecule and I'm like a tree. Well, I don't know what we are. I am so not a science nerd. We're different. You don't hang out with people who are different than you. 4-H'ers hang with 4-H'ers. Cheerleaders with cheerleaders. Geeks with geeks. There's a whole group of supersmart science kids in the junior class.

It may not look so separated to you, Sheriff, because everyone from Fred High is here looking for Tommy. But that's because this is a small town and we all show up when something bad happens, but I bet people are grouped up out there. You know, walking the Stillwell Ranch with their same group of friends.

It's not a bad thing. People sticking with their same interest group. It's more peaceful. People are happier. Even new kids know that. Like there was this new girl. Leann something. A senior. Can you imagine transferring someplace new your senior year? Anyway, you could tell right away she was this kind of loner person. Like she didn't fit in. Well, guess who she is hanging out with? The only senior going to an art school. Mary Louise. See? Even the loners stick with loners.

I'm really sorry, Sheriff Caldwell. I talk a lot when I'm nervous and I guess talking to you and being the last person to see Tommy makes me nervous.

Unhappy? Tommy? I don't think so. Why would he be unhappy about being in the science nerd group if that's who he was? He seemed like a regular nerd. Always reading. Or writing in that notebook. Probably about his scientific discoveries. Isn't that how nerds act? All kind of preoccupied with things they're thinking about?

We mostly crossed paths in the library. That's where I had my Latinitas meetings. It's a group I started for all the Mexican girls at Fred. Like a support group. Anyway, whenever we sat near Tommy, he was always by himself writing or studying. As soon as we sat down, he jumped up and walked away really fast, stuffing his books and notebook and pencils in his backpack as he went. We weren't being loud or talking about dumb stuff. I don't know. Maybe he was late for something. Or maybe he didn't like being too near us. Whatever. My point is it looked like he'd rather be alone.

Withdrawn? Maybe. But I don't really know, right? Cuz I don't hang out with the science nerds. Not even the girl nerds. Two of the nerdiest ones are in my class. Izzy and Rachel. They're part of the whole junior nerd squad. Like they're already in AP physics B, which is a senior class. Izzy seems nice. She tutors in my pre-AP physics class. She's hitting on one of the guys. Tim. He's a total jock. Talk about mismatched.

I don't know if Tommy had a girlfriend. I doubt it. I saw Rachel get on the back of his bike once or twice. She wasn't with him on Friday though. It didn't look like a girlfriend thing. I mean, he didn't smile at her or have his arm around her. But I don't know. Maybe nerd boyfriends act like that. Which is why I wouldn't be interested in any of the science nerds as boyfriends. Even the illustrious James Houghton. Total eye candy. But really snobby.

James thinks we should be in separate groups because he doesn't want to dilute his gene pool. I'm serious. He's a total segregationist. He wrote about it in the Fred newspaper. He says his IQ is a 140 and he won't go out with anyone less than a 120. James thinks cheerleaders and football players are holding back evolution. As if. Cheerleaders are *not* stupid. I told James he sounded like a Nazi. You know, very Final Solution. I think he was surprised I got up in his face, like there's more to me than pom-poms.

That's why I started Latinitas. I want to be a cheerleader. I want to go to college. I want to study history and political science and economics. I want to do a lot of things. But sometimes when you're Hispanic, people think all you can do is have babies. Especially Mexicans. You know, we're the house cleaners, the ditch diggers, and the crop pickers. I used to say that I was Hispanic. But after I went online and read about other Latinitas groups, I started thinking about how I didn't say I was Mexican. Like I didn't want to claim it. Now I do. Not a lot of girls have joined, but maybe when I'm a senior next year more girls will. Like I'll be more of a role model. I don't know. It's hard to break out of a stereotype and be different. I guess that's why people hide out in groups, you know?

Tommy was definitely weird. Not in a creepy way. In a really awkward way. Like he was tuned into another frequency. I mean, I've been in school with him since middle grade and he was always the weird nerdy kid. But not like an outcast. Just awkward, really awkward. Like one time I was ahead of him in the lunch line and I dropped my spork. It landed right near his foot and all he did was stare at it like it fell from some other planet. I finally picked it up and all he said was, "I wonder if that fell through a wormhole."

That's how he was. Or is. Like you couldn't have a conversation with him because he was thinking about esoteric stuff all the time. Or I couldn't. I mean, I talk a lot, right? My best friend Tara says that I sound a little ditzy because of the way I talk about everything all over the place. But I'm not ditzy, right? I'm smart. I have a 3.98 GPA and my IQ meets the James Houghton standard, but like I never talked with Tommy because he didn't talk like I talk. You know?

I probably shouldn't refer to him in the past tense. I mean, he's only been missing for three days. Do you think Tommy could be dead? Wouldn't that be creepy awful if I was the last person to see Tommy alive? Like maybe if I'd waved or stopped or talked to him, you wouldn't be interviewing me about Tommy. Like something might have changed if we'd done one thing different before. You know?

All possibilities exist.

When I make an observation, all possibilities collapse into one. The other possibilities don't disappear. Instead, their probability of existence is transferred from them to the only remaining possibility.

If we can only observe this universe, it doesn't mean that other universes don't exist. They do. But our observation disrupts the possibility of multiple universes so that they collapse into the only one we can observe.

So, is it our observation that limits possibility?

What about imagination? If I can imagine parallel universes, why can't I observe them?

Maybe imagination is a less disruptive form of observation.

Maybe if we really imagine what's possible, then stepping into another dimension or a parallel universe will be like crossing the street.

THE PROPOSAL

MARSHALL STEERS THE LUMBERING STATION wagon past the edge of the pull-out behind the cactus and scrub cedar. He turns off the car and opens the windows. No one can see his car tucked back here. At twilight, behind the cedars, it's like the gathering shadows swallow him. With everybody looking for Tommy Smythe this past week, it's been hard to come out. Now that the big search teams have left, it's finally quiet again. He closes his eyes and tunes his ears to the sounds outside his car. First, a few birds chirrup. Then there's a rustling. Maybe an armadillo is creeping under the brush. Last, a breeze. Marshall can hear it stir through the trees before it creeps inside his car. Always the air moves out here even when it's dead still in town.

As soon as his grandfather gave him the old station wagon last year, Marshall drove around looking for someplace quiet. When he stopped in the pull-out near the Stillwell Ranch, he noticed a break in the cedars at one end of it. At first, he thought maybe he shouldn't let the branches scratch the sides of the car, until he realized there were already so many dings and scratches on it a few more wouldn't matter. He likes to think out here. Sometimes at school—people, gossip, drama—it all comes at him too fast. Out here, he can slow it down, think about what each person said, how they looked when they said it. Out here, he can think about Leann.

Asking Leann to the prom a month ago had been the easy part. All he had to do was bring it up at lunch when he was sitting with Leann, Robert, and Mary Louise. All he had to do was bring it up casually.

First, he pointed to the poster announcing the prom like he'd seen it for the first time. Then he said, "Hey, this is our last chance to go to prom. Why don't we all go together?"

Once they were all like, "Cool idea," he brought up the next part.

It was a little trickier.

"What do you say we go together, but as dates? Like, I'll take Leann. Robert and Mary Louise can go together."

Leann sounded suspicious. "Why would we want to do that?"

Marshall was prepared. He rocked back on the cafeteria bench and shrugged his shoulders. Then he looked into her eyes. Her translucent blue eyes. "Because it's prom. We should have the full prom experience. You know, tuxedoes and corsages. It doesn't mean we're going to be romantic. But why not go for the full-meal deal?" Marshall made sure his tone wasn't defensive. He couldn't sound like he wanted the corsage or the tuxedo. Even though he did.

Marshall knew Mary Louise would go for it right away. "I think it sounds awesome. We could be prom pretenders. We'd get the experience without getting all weird and nervous."

"But we're the ones who have to shell out the money for the corsage and the tuxedo," Robert said.

That's when Leann jumped in and backhanded Robert on the shoulder. "Quit whining, Robert. You think I have a prom dress hanging in my closet? This sounds weird enough to be fun. Let's do it. You and me, Marshall, the prom pretenders."

Marshall couldn't have planned Robert's reaction any better. He was usually negative about spending money. As for Leann, he'd seen her counter Robert's resistance before. Her hesitation about all things social seemed to evaporate when Robert dragged his cleats outside anything athletic. Pushing him moved her.

Marshall smiled. Not too big. Just a slight upturn on one side of his lips and then he grabbed the apple from his lunch tray and took a big bite, saying, "Cool," as he chewed. Getting her to come out here after the prom might be a little more difficult.

At least it's going to happen. When that Tommy kid disappeared a week ago, a few parents wanted to cancel it. But some PhD psychologist from Austin who came out to help with the search said it was important to keep life as normal as possible for everyone. Besides, Fred High's tradition of having prom on the Saturday before Mother's Day is pretty twisted. It's not like anyone can stay out all night if you have to wish your mom a happy Mother's Day the very next day.

Leann had never said anything about her mother. Marshall asked her once if she moved here with her family and the question made her look angry, as if a storm had blown into her light blue eyes. All she said was, "I live with my aunt." Marshall knew enough not to ask another question. Ever since, he's noticed she has these dark places that make her shut down. That's why bringing her out here is so important.

Marshall opens his eyes and looks out at the night. Between now and when prom happens in two days, he'll figure out how to get her here. Turning the key in the ignition, Marshall presses the gas until the engine chugs and turns over with a roar, silencing all the night sounds. He maneuvers the car through the cedars, across the pull-out, and back onto US 281. Marshall wishes the car would go faster, as if its speed would get him to Saturday night more quickly. He wants everything to go perfectly. He's wanted everything to go perfectly from the day Leann started Fredrick Johnson High last August.

Usually the first day of school is a parade of everyone trying to show off and make the best first impression. Not Leann Jordan. When she showed up in McCloud's first period astronomy class, it seemed like she didn't care how she looked. Her long, almost-black hair was, well, messy. And a little greasy. It sort of hung limp, close to her cheeks, nearly covering her eyes. McCloud assigned her the seat next to Marshall and he could see she was watching everyone from behind the dark strands.

When she said her name in class and where she came from—Midland—she didn't offer up any more information. She didn't giggle or smile or do anything that looked like she wanted a friend or that she wanted to be liked. Even her T-shirts were dark and baggy, like she was covering up her body. She looked like she wanted to fade into the background.

Marshall wondered if she didn't want to be noticed on purpose. He wondered if she was scared. Or shy and quiet. Maybe she was waiting to see who she could trust. He watched her. He wanted her to trust him. Marshall wanted to protect her. He'd never felt like that about any girl. A week after school started, no more dirty or messy hair, but it hung in her face like she still was hiding. Two weeks later, she wore a light blue T-shirt. It almost hugged her waist.

. . . . .

Leann slumped in her seat. She shouldn't have worn this shirt. It was too revealing. She felt like she had a neon sign pointing at her. Boys were going to notice her. Again. She fought the urge to jump up and leave Mr. McCloud's class. If she went home and changed now, she'd really draw attention to herself. She stayed put. She kept her head down and tried to concentrate on what McCloud was saying. He was handing back their quizzes. When he stood in front of her desk, Leann glanced up and took the quiz from his hand. "100" was circled at the top of the page. She heard him say "Nice work." Leann nodded but didn't look in his eyes.

Then McCloud said "Nice work" again and Leann wondered if he was still talking to her. She looked up. He wasn't. He was talking to the guy who sat next to her. She glanced to the right and saw "100" at the top of his quiz. She read the name next to the grade. Marshall Johnson. She didn't want to look at his face but she was curious to see who else had aced the quiz. She glanced up. Long enough to notice that he wore rimless glasses and his eyes were hazel. Long enough to feel her cheeks prickle with heat. Then she looked away.

. . . . .

Marshall hoped the 100 would get her attention. He'd noticed she got perfect scores on every quiz so far. Someone who was smart might be curious about other people with good grades. When McCloud handed him the quiz with 100 circled at the top, it seemed like a sign. Marshall left it faceup on his desk. He felt her look at him but he kept staring ahead as if McCloud were imparting the secrets of the astronomic universe. Really, Marshall was counting how long she looked at him. One one thousand, Two one thousand, Three—

Almost three seconds. She'd noticed him.

After that, Marshall still kept to himself, but one time he looked at her as she sat down and she said, "Hey." He nodded at her. Marshall was careful to hold back. He didn't want to scare her away. She seemed like she could be easily scared.

One day at the end of class, she said, "See you tomorrow." After a while, she said "Hey" every morning. Once, she double-checked her homework assignment with what he wrote down.

In January, Marshall noticed she came into the cafeteria with Mary Louise. That was odd because Mary Louise usually ate in the art room. Painting was her life. She was the only person in the senior class going to an art school. It seemed like another sign. When Robert put his tray down across from

Marshall, he said, "You mind if I invite Mary Louise over to eat with us?"

Robert looked over at the cafeteria line. "She's sort of a wing nut."

"Yeah, and you're sort of a jock. So what?"

"Sure. Why not? It'll be a change from listening to you talk about colleges."

Marshall ignored Robert. He did talk a lot about where he might go to college. It seemed important, but at the same time, it didn't. He was good at math and the counselor said that engineering would be a good fit, so he applied to colleges that had engineering programs. He'd been accepted at three and chose one. But he still wasn't sure if he wanted to go. It was simpler for Robert. All he wanted to do was play football, so he took the best deal.

Marshall waved at Mary Louise as she was scanning the lunchroom for a seat. She smiled and tried to wave but nearly dropped her tray.

"Wing nut," mumbled Robert.

Mary Louise leaned toward Leann and sort of pointed at Marshall and Robert. Marshall could see Leann hesitate. Her eyes scanned the room, looking for another possibility. But there weren't any empty tables. She nodded and followed Mary Louise.

Marshall made sure to motion to the seat next to him when Mary Louise came up to the table. He didn't want to spook Leann.

"Y'all know Leann?" Mary Louise said as she slid her tray next to Marshall's. "We have gym together."

Marshall nodded. "Yeah, we have astronomy together." He motioned to Robert as Leann sat down. "This is Robert. Mostly a jock. Also a good friend."

Leann smiled a little. Marshall wasn't sure why but he had a feeling that she liked this strange crew. The jock. The artist. The engineer. And whoever Leann was. Marshall also had a feeling that because there were four of them together, it made Leann more comfortable. Like one on one, even with Mary Louise, would be too close.

Marshall didn't mind. He liked that Mary Louise and Robert were there. It helped him blend in better. He could pretend to be eating while listening to them talk. Listening to Leann talk. Listening to how she feinted and dodged but never really opened up. She made it seem like she was there, a part of them, but Marshall sensed she was someplace else.

·   · · · · ·

Leann takes out her mascara and rolls it on her eyelashes. She still can't believe she's going to prom. Eight months ago, she wondered if it were possible to live someplace and not know anyone the entire time you lived there. Maybe she could hold her breath for a whole school year and not talk to anyone. It turned out she couldn't. Something happens. You forget your gym shorts and you have to borrow some. After that, Mary Louise—the girl with the extra shorts—says something to you every day. Something nice. Not very prying. You wonder about her paint-splotched fingers. She tells you more about herself. You find yourself liking not being alone. Pretty soon you go to lunch with her and then you're sitting with two guys and presto you're going to the prom. Maybe it's the perfect thing to do to finish off this exile from her life back in Midland. A prom. A step toward normal. With friends. No romance. A sort of date with Marshall. A sort of date would be all right. With Marshall.

She still wasn't sure about him. He looked like a dangerous combination of smart and sensitive. She liked smart because she hated dumb. But smart meant she had to be watchful. Smart meant someone could pull a fast one on her. Smart meant she wasn't sure she could trust him.

Sensitive confused her. She thought he was sensitive. Maybe it was his eyes. Or those glasses. They made him look vulnerable. Breakable. Maybe it was the way he didn't push himself at her. He couldn't hurt her if he was sensitive. Could he?

It couldn't hurt her to go to the prom with a pretend date. Could it?

Leann was never sure what would hurt. It was like her antenna mixed all the signals up when someone got close. She couldn't figure out what they wanted. Or she did know what they wanted and it was wrong but they said they loved her so it couldn't be wrong. But it was her uncle so it was wrong but he said he loved her so maybe it wasn't. Then it was her cousin but he said he loved her so maybe it wasn't but it was. It *was* wrong. Every time. But they said they loved her. They said so. Then her mother found out and said Leann was a "little tease, the kind of girl that gets boys in trouble." She sent Leann away. "Go live with my sister. See if she can teach you to keep your hands to yourself."

The night before she left, her cousin whispered at her door, "Wanna suck me off one more time?" Leann didn't move. She wasn't sure what she should do. She thought she should go to the door. He was always nice to her afterwards. She could hear him breathing. Then he kicked the door and said "Bitch." Leann gripped the edge of her bed and held her breath. She felt guilty. Maybe she should have opened the door. Whenever he got angry, she felt like she should have done something different.

When her aunt picked her up at the bus station in Fredericksburg, she didn't ask what happened. She never pried. She let Leann be. After a month or so, Leann relaxed enough to take her first big breath of air. Then a second and a third.

Now it's time for the prom and she is almost breathing like normal again.

. . . . .

When Marshall pulls up in front of Leann's house, he has to remind himself this is pretend. It isn't really a date. He can hardly believe that yesterday he convinced all of them that picking up their date was part of the ritual, even for pretend dates.

"How about we meet Mary Louise and Robert outside the dance in the parking lot and walk in together," he'd said to Leann.

Leann didn't like the idea. "This sounds more and more like a real prom date. I think we should all go together."

Marshall shrugged. "Okay. Then I want to be the driver."

"No way," said Robert. "I want my own ride."

"I get carsick if I ride in the back," Mary Louise added.

"Okay, I get it," said Leann. "No one wants to be the cute couple in the back seat."

Marshall wouldn't have minded playing the part of the cute

couple, but driving all together would have made coming out to the pull-out at the end of the night more difficult.

Walking up to Leann's door, Marshall composes himself. As soon as he knocks, an older woman answers. She has Leann's long dark hair but it's streaked with gray.

"My name is Marshall Johnson. I'm here to take Leann to the prom."

"I'm Leann's aunt. Jackie." She reaches out and Marshall shakes her hand. It feels callused like a man's. It's strange to hold this hand and stare into a face that looks like an older version of Leann. Then Leann appears. Standing next to her aunt, it looks as if time had split their cells. Neither smiles. Both have that same wariness in their eyes. Except Leann is beautiful. Her blue dress is dusted with silver so that it looks as translucent as her eyes.

When Leann steps toward him, Marshall sucks in his breath and holds it. He almost exhales an audible "Ahhh," but he doesn't slip up. He holds it together as they walk to his car and he opens the door for her.

. . . . .

Leann sits straight up. Her back barely touches the passenger seat of Marshall's car. She reaches for the door handle. She could run back inside. She could tell him she has food poisoning. She could fake stomach heaves. She could . . .

She holds on to the cold metal handle. Breathing. Holding on to the door handle calms her. If anything bad happens, she can open the door and fling herself out. Even if it's moving. When Marshall sits down, she glances over at him. He doesn't look any different, right? He hasn't done anything wrong, right? It's a fake date, right?

. . . . .

Marshall doesn't know what to do. Leann looks a little ill. Should he notice? Should he say something? If he were a boyfriend, he'd say something. What would a fake date do?

"Oh, I got a corsage for you." Marshall tries to sound as off-hand as possible, pointing at the plastic box on the dashboard. "They're gardenias. I wasn't sure what color dress you would wear so I got a white flower. To go with anything." Only they aren't meant to go with anything. They are meant for her. He wants her to have those beautiful white flowers wrapped around her wrist all night. He wants her to remember him whenever she smells a gardenia.

Marshall watches Leann open the box and stare at the corsage. He can hear her take a short sip of air as if smelling the flowers might hurt her. Then it sounds like she stops breathing altogether. Marshall isn't sure if he should start the car or not. She looks like she might puke. Marshall scrambles. "I hope you like it. It was weird bringing it. I got a little nervous. I worried if you would like it. This pretend stuff started to feel a little real, ya know?"

. . . . .

Leann laughs. A short, sharp "Hah" pops out of her mouth. It surprises her. Like the breath she was holding exploded out of her. Her laugh must have surprised Marshall. He jumps as if she had scared him. That makes her laugh more. She loosens her grip on the door handle. She's glad he's nervous too. Hearing him say it makes her relax.

"Yeah, a little too real."

"Maybe it's the corsage. You don't have to wear it."

Leann takes the corsage out of the box and puts it around her wrist. She stretches her arm in front of her and looks at the bracelet of white petals. "No, I want to wear it. It's beautiful."

"Good. I mean, let's—I mean, it doesn't mean anything. They're just flowers. It's tradition, right?"

"Right." Leann raises the white flowers to her nose, breathes in their fragrance, and leans back onto the seat.

· · · · ·

Marshall circles the Fred High parking lot, looking for Robert's truck. He sees it parked in the far corner of the lot. Robert is sitting on the tailgate. The cab windows are open and the twang of Robert's favorite country and western station accompanies Mary Louise as she twirls around in an empty parking space next to the truck. She looks like a ballerina. Even her skirt is a white net material.

"We saved you a spot." Mary Louise stops twirling and jumps out of the way. "Actually, I saved you a spot. Robert wouldn't dance with me. He thought it was too goofy to dance in a parking lot."

"Hell, yes," says Robert. He clicks off his radio. "It's already pretty goofy I spent twenty bucks on a damn corsage and another ten on this tuxedo from Goodwill for a pretend date."

"Ooooh . . . you're lucky, Mary Louise," says Leann, admiring the bridge of sweetheart roses circling her wrist. "He spent more on your corsage than his tuxedo."

Leann and Mary Louise laugh and head toward the gym. Marshall trails behind with Robert. "Phew, that tuxedo stinks."

"Shit," says Robert. "I dumped a whole bottle of Old Spice on it."

"Yeah, now it smells like cinnamon-spiced cat pee."

"Shit. I swear it didn't smell at Goodwill."

"Mary Louise didn't say anything?"

"Naw, she's too nice. Do you think I should change? I've got some jeans in the truck. The shirt doesn't smell bad. It's my dad's."

Marshall weighs Robert's question. He'd gotten them to the prom. Leann was his date. It didn't really matter if Robert dressed the part. "Yeah, smelling like cat pee is a really bad idea."

Robert lopes back to his truck. "Tell Mary Louise I'll be there in a minute."

Leann and Mary Louise grab a table close to the dance floor. They wave to Marshall. As he walks up, the band starts playing a fast song. On impulse, Marshall takes both girls by the arm onto the dance floor. When Robert comes in, Leann pulls him into their circle. After a few fast songs, the band slows down. Marshall wants to ask Leann but he has to pretend this isn't a date. He takes Mary Louise by the hand and bows. "May I have this dance?" Mary Louise giggles and nods. As they dance away from Leann and Robert, Marshall forces himself not to look at Leann. He pretends he wants to slow dance with Mary Louise first.

· · · · ·

Leann looks over at Robert to see if he is going to ask her to slow dance. As he turns to go back to the table, Leann feels disappointed. She's enjoying herself. More than she thought she would.

She grabs Robert by his elbow and pulls him onto the dance floor. "Come on."

Robert moans. "I hate this song."

"Tough. This is our prom. We're dancing."

"Can't we pretend dance?"

"You want me to pretend slap you?" Leann raises her hand above Robert's shoulder.

Robert groans. Leann smiles. She doesn't have to pretend. She's having fun.

· · · · ·

Marshall dances every dance. When he slow dances with Leann, he doesn't let himself relax. He keeps thinking of things to talk about. What he really wants to do is concentrate on how one of her hands cups his shoulder and the other hooks around his thumb.

One time, when all four of them are dancing together, sort of jumping in a circle, Leann leans in close to Marshall. "Thanks.

This is great." Then she smiles. Marshall stops dancing for a second. He can smell the gardenias, the sweetness hanging between them. He wants to kiss her. Her cheek is an inch from his lips. He stops himself. "You're welcome," he says close to her ear. Then he jumps away from how perilously close he is to the edge of her and keeps dancing, glancing over again and again, hoping she didn't notice that the mask he is wearing had slipped for an instant.

· · · · ·

Leann barely hears Marshall say "You're welcome."

She's laughing. For the first time in a long time, she is really laughing. When the band takes a break, she goofs around at their table, thumb wrestling each of them and winning against everyone except Robert, whose big hand engulfs hers. Even then, she pretends to win by using both hands, claiming her two hands are equal in size to his one. Mary Louise suggests they all get their picture taken together and Leann helps arrange the photo so they are all squished together. When she poses with Marshall as a couple, she doesn't think twice about his arm looped in hers.

When the prom ends and Marshall suggests they go to the Whip In, Leann doesn't hesitate. She wants to keep having fun. Pretty soon this guy named Sam, who everyone but Leann seems to know, is taking their orders. Fifteen minutes later, burgers, fries, and sodas fill their table.

Ravenous, sweaty from dancing, Leann guzzles her Dr Pepper and burps so loud both Marshall and Robert choke on their burgers in shock while she and Mary Louise fall over in their seats, holding their sides.

"Holy crap," said Robert. "That sounded like a whale burp."

"Do whales burp?" asked Mary Louise.

"If they did, it would sound like that," said Robert.

Leann smiles. Having Robert make a joke at her expense doesn't bother her. She sniffs her gardenia corsage. "I wonder where this corsage tradition came from."

Mary Louise waves her hand in front of her nose and smells her corsage. "To cover up their date's stinky tuxedo smell."

"Hey, that's in the car."

"Still too close."

They fall into laughing again. Mary Louise never insulted anyone.

"I have the receipt. I bet I can return it."

"No way," says Marshall. "You'll have to donate it back to Goodwill."

"You might have to pay them to take it," Mary Louise adds, and they start laughing again.

· · · · ·

Outside the Whip In, Marshall hopes Leann will walk straight to his car but she doesn't. Mary Louise stops to look at the poster of Tommy Smythe on the window.

"It's so sad," says Mary Louise. "He was a really nice kid."

Leann stops next to her. "Do you think he is dead?"

"I don't know. It's been like eight days."

"Eight days is nothing out here," says Robert. "He could definitely show up still."

Marshall doesn't say anything. Ever since that kid went missing, it seems like Tommy is trying to jinx Marshall's plans for the evening. First he put the prom in doubt and then he made it more difficult to take Leann to the pull-out because the sheriff drives out there more often. Normally, Marshall wouldn't wish harm on anyone but, in this case, he really would have preferred Tommy's body being found. With Mary Louise feeling sad and Leann not moving, Marshall is wondering how to break the spell and move the evening forward.

"Hey, prom pretenders, shall we take our fake dates home?" Marshall doesn't feel as offhand as he hoped he sounded.

Mary Louise looks at her watch. "Oh yeah, my sisters and I are cooking breakfast for Mom in the morning."

"Oh crap, I forgot about Mother's Day," said Robert.

Leann laughs. "Don't worry, Robert, if you remember to say anything tomorrow, she'll be surprised."

"You think?" said Robert.

"Definitely," says Leann, laughing. "See you at school on Monday."

Just like that, Marshall is holding the car door open for Leann. She doesn't look bothered by the whole Tommy thing. Or the mention of Mother's Day. He takes a deep breath. Here's the big moment. He is scared. What if she says no? Except they'd had a good time. Why not go ahead and say it?

"Leann, can I show you something before I take you home?"

"Sure."

It's that easy. Minutes later, he is turning his car off 281. Marshall scans the pull-out. No cars. He slows down and heads the car toward one end of the pull-out. In the dark, it looks like he is driving straight into a wall of trees. He eases the car through the cedars, tensing a little until his headlights stretch into the field beyond. No matter how many times he drives through the gauntlet of trees, it's hard not to imagine a cliff beyond the cedars. He drives about ten feet into the field, turns off the car, and rolls down his window.

"People call this place the Stillwell pull-out."

. . . . .

As soon as Marshall turns off the car and opens the window, Leann can feel the night air crawl in and cover her. She glances over at Marshall and reaches for the door handle. His head is tipped back and his eyes are closed.

"Close your eyes and listen. It's amazing."

She isn't going to close her eyes. Ever.

"Here." Marshall reaches over and cranks open Leann's window.

Leann flinches and presses back into the seat away from his arm.

. . . . .

Something is wrong. Why is she grabbing the door handle and jumping like he is going to hurt her? This isn't what he wanted.

"No, wait, Leann. I didn't bring you here to kiss you. Or do anything. Honest."

Leann's hand doesn't move away from the handle.

"I wanted you to see this place. Hear it. I like to come out here and open the windows and sit and listen. Sometimes I look at the stars for our class." Marshall stops. He doesn't want to use this many words to explain this place but he feels like she might open the door and walk away if he doesn't keep talking.

"There used to be a house straight out from here. A couple of hundred yards. The old Stillwell place. I went out there to look for that kid Tommy Smythe. Right after he disappeared. Not with the search parties. I thought maybe he might be there. I don't know. Hiding out. No one knows why he disappeared. I thought maybe something bad had happened and he needed to get away. That's what I would do."

Leann isn't saying a word. Marshall can barely hear her breathing. He can smell the gardenias. The sticky sweetness smells out of place in the cedar-tinged night air.

"Anyway, I went out there. He wasn't there. And neither was the house, hardly. It looked like the wind and animals, even the insects, had taken it back."

Marshall looks out the window, past Leann's frozen profile. The misshapen moon drifts out from behind a cloud and catches a bleached rock in its gaze. This isn't what he wanted to be talking about. Insects. Tommy. Decaying houses.

"Leann, I need to tell you the truth. Is that all right? Can I tell you the truth?" Marshall waits for her to answer but she doesn't. "I noticed you right away. I saw you on the first day of school last August and I, well, I wanted to bring you here the minute I saw you. I noticed how quiet you were. I thought you would like it here."

Now that he isn't angling to get behind her defenses, he's lost. He thought she would understand this place. He thought she would understand the silence. He thought about starting the car and going back, but he can't give up. Yet.

"Everybody at Fred High thinks they're going to be something someday. Like Robert wants to play pro football and Mary Louise wants to be a famous artist. That's what we're there for, right? To learn a bunch of stuff so we can be more than who we are. But what if we get jobs and get married and have kids and grandkids and then die? What if all we're supposed to do is be happy with that? Do you know what I am saying? Leann?"

Leann doesn't move. Marshall is running out of words. He can't see what he is doing wrong.

"I mean, I'll probably go to college and do something, I don't know, engineering, teaching. But then I come out here and I think, what if I just loved someone? What if that was it? What if all I did was be a good husband. A good provider. What if, when the wind and bugs erased me, that was all I'd done: loved one person? Wouldn't that be good enough?" Marshall is saying all the words he had dreamed of saying to her, but instead of weaving some beautiful picture, they are falling in a mess on the seat of the car.

Marshall reaches toward Leann. She flinches and presses her body closer to the door. Instead of touching her, his hand falls empty.

. . . . .

Leann isn't sure if she should open the door and run. She tries to find the edge of her skin where it touches the night air, the seat, and the door. He keeps talking to her, pelting words at her.

Leann is counting each breath of air. In between, she can hear Marshall's words. "I would love you, I swear." Six breaths. "I thought you would understand . . ." Marshall's voice trails off. Five breaths.

Leann swallows another sip of air and holds it hard inside her. *Love.* The word drips like the remains of semen down the back of her throat. She stares ahead, but in her periphery, she can tell Marshall hasn't moved. She pushes out the words. "Take me home."

. . . . .

Marshall looks at her profile. The way the shadows cut across her face, it looks like her mouth and her jawline are lopped off. He wants to believe she hasn't said those words. If he can't see her mouth, maybe she hasn't said them. Maybe it's the quiet playing tricks on him. Or the wind.

What did he do wrong? He was so careful. He'd picked a girl who is shy and quiet and looks like she needs protection. Isn't this where he reveals himself and she is supposed to understand him? Isn't this place meant to bring them together?

Then he hears. "Please."

Marshall rolls up his window. The smell of gardenias fills his nostrils. Even though he can't see them, Marshall knows the bright white petals have turned yellow. He starts the car and turns around in the field. He thinks he sees a javelina standing stock-still and raises his arm to point it out to Leann. But when he looks again, it's gone. He lowers his arm and grips the steering wheel. He has no more words.

· · · · ·

Leann stares ahead. She doesn't roll up her window. The wind blows over her. She shivers a little. Her hair whips across her face. She likes how the strands of hair lash at her. Until she sees the moon. Then she reaches up with one hand and holds her hair back so she can watch it float next to them. When it slips behind a cloud, she wishes with all her heart it would come back out.

Sometimes I think this world—the one we are living in right now—is the one where we have to get it right. It's like we're in this test place where we are figuring stuff out. Like the physicists are figuring out about how the universe started; doctors are figuring out how the body heals itself; ecologists are figuring out how to bring the earth back into balance.

Maybe this is the knowledge portal and the parallel universes are the imagination portals. Once we step through the imagination portal, we don't have to struggle with good or bad. Everything just is. Even this world. Maybe we can even see it from the parallel universes. Like it's in an old movie theater and we can go take a look at it every once in a while to remember what we left behind. But after a while we stop going, because we don't need that knowledge anymore. Everything we imagine is possible, including who we are and where we are.

ALVIN

HEY, QUIT SHINING THAT FUCKING LIGHT IN MY eyes.

What? Do I look like I fucking went to a prom tonight?

My license and registration? What for? Is stopping here illegal or something? All I was doing was sitting here. Besides, I don't have to give it to you. I looked it up online.

My hands *are* on the fucking wheel. I asked you a question, doughnut hole. Why can't I fucking sit here?

No way. I'm not getting out of my car. I'm not doing anything wrong. I'm just sitting here. I swear. What's the problem with that?

You get to ask all the questions? No wonder people fucking hate cops.

No way. I am not getting out. I wasn't doing anything wrong. I was sitting here. That's all. No weed. No booze.

Hey, wait, you can't fucking open my door without permission. What are you arresting me for? What the fuck?! Shit. This door doesn't have a handle. Hey, let me out! You can't search my car without a warrant. Hey!

Okay, if you fuck with me, I'm gonna—

Ow! Shit! Ow! Shit! Ow! Damnit! Hey, Captain Cruller, I'm bleeding. "Yes, Your Honor. All I was doing was sitting in the pull-out and this cop beat the shit out of me. He kept smashing me in the head." Ow!

I knew that would make you stop. Hey. Wait. What's with the handcuffs?

Stop looking at my back. Quit lifting up my shirt. I don't care if you tie me up, I'll still bash my head on this door. And with my other bruises, you'll lose your fucking job.

Hey, wait a minute. Where are we going? You can't leave my car like that. Please, man. That's my ride. At least take the keys out of it so no one will steal it. Please. That's my way out, man. Please. I'll answer your questions, okay? Please . . .

Thanks.

Yeah, I'm Alvin Clark. My dad owns the salvage yard. The one and only.

Shit happens. You get banged up working in the yard. It's not a big deal.

Yeah, he hits me. So what? I was doing something stupid. Who knows? I probably deserved it.

Right. Parents aren't supposed to hit kids. Not in my world. My old man owns a fucking salvage yard. There's a two-hour window after he drinks his first beer every day that he likes me. Three beers later, I'm a worthless piece of shit. Maybe some parents don't hit their kids. But not mine. I'm living a fucking stereotype.

Yeah, I work for him. I pull shit apart that comes in the yard. I know where everything is. I paid him for every bolt on that car. Yeah. I put it together. Two years of working for free to pay for it. Longer. Because it took me a while to figure out when to do the accounts. It couldn't be too early in the morning because if he had a hangover, he'd get pissed and charge me more or tell me I hadn't worked enough. And it couldn't be too late 'cause then he wouldn't remember.

Fucking asshole.

Mom? Long gone. I was ten. She disappeared.

Naw, he never reported it. She left and he started doing the cooking.

I used to wonder if he killed her and buried her out back but all her clothes were gone. So she must have taken them. If he killed her, the clothes would still be there or he would have sold 'em.

Because that's the way he is. Everything needs to earn their way or they are a worthless piece of shit. If the dog doesn't bark when someone sets foot in the yard, bam! If the cat doesn't kill the rats, bam!

Oh yeah, it's Mother's Day, isn't it? Happy fucking Mother's Day.

So where you taking me? Jail? What? We're gonna drive around? That's what I was out doing. I stopped at the pull-out because, well, they said that's where they found Tommy's bike and I didn't get to go on all the searches last week. He really liked that bike. I thought I'd stop and see if, I don't know, maybe there were some clues.

He and his dad bought that bike out at the yard. Tommy came out a couple of times afterwards and asked me to fix some stuff. One time the headlight wouldn't work. Another time, let's see . . . Oh yeah, I had to replace the brake cable and pads. The pads looked like he'd taken a sander to them, but I'd seen the way he drove. Fuckin' nut. If there was anyone who needed heavy-duty brake pads, it was Tommy. Drove crazy fast and then jammed on the brakes. Not to show off. He stopped and looked at shit. It's a good thing I sold him the bike with brand-new tires. The old man wanted me to put on used ones but I told him I put on new ones and charged him double. I could lie to him about shit like that if he'd started his second six-pack.

I liked Tommy. I didn't know him. I mean, we talked when he came out to the yard. He was weird, man. He'd ask me the strangest shit. Like I remember one time I was showing him how I organized the yard. All the Japanese parts in one place. By year. It made sense to me. When you're building your own car, you want to know shit like that. Anyway, he asked me if you lived in a dimension where there was no time, would all the cars work with the same parts. Like there wouldn't be years and so there wouldn't be makes or models or crap like that. The dude could think up some weird shit.

He told me that time travel was totally possible. Like through wormholes. He said they already exist on a subatomic level. I told him if that was possible, would he mind looking for a 1980 Trans Am carburetor. I got one from a Chevy V8 and it doesn't work like I want. He got like really serious and said he couldn't do it because he couldn't go back to a time before the wormhole machine was created. So I said, maybe he could figure out a way to jump time without a machine. And he was like, "Yeah, maybe."

Hey, man, I mean, Sheriff, do you think you could stop and take off these handcuffs? They hurt like shit. I promise I won't do anything. Hey, thanks. It's not like I could go anywhere. Where are we? Oh, right, the Simmons place is over that way. You know, you should check that guy out. I don't think he's only farming lavender, if you know what I mean. Well, he drives that Super Glide Harley for one thing. Plus, I know his daughter Tara's in my class and she says he goes away a lot. Real farmers don't do that: disappear for long stretches.

I don't think Tommy went into another dimension like the way kids at school are saying he did. I don't know if it could happen but sometimes the way Tommy showed up, it was like he'd dropped out of another time and space.

Like one time, at the yard, he appeared, out of the blue. It was probably six months ago. Maybe more. My old man didn't even see him. It was a good thing, too. He was pissed. On his third six-pack and using me for target practice. Not really. Every once in a while, he'd make me set up targets in the yard. For kicks. Beer cans. Broken tools. It started one day, years ago, when this fucking tape measure wouldn't snap back. Pissed him off. He went in the shop and got a gun. Set the tape measure up on top of a barrel. He was laughing like crazy. He got all the other tape measures out and set them up where he was working and then he started yelling at them, "This is what happens when you don't work right." Pow. The broken tape measure flew in the air. He shot it again, right where it landed.

"This is what happens to lousy tools." Bam. Bam. Bam. That tape measure had so many fucking holes.

But you know what? That day, my old man was fucking laughing. He never laughs.

He's a welder. He can make two pieces of metal look like one. It's tricky. Too much heat and the sheet metal will warp. Too little heat and it's a weak weld. Somehow he knew the right amount of heat. But if something didn't work, he'd fucking lose it. That day Tommy showed up, he was losing it bad. A clamp slipped and he torched the edge of a sheet. It was toast. Never fucking occurred to him to drink less. That maybe he was too plowed to tighten the clamp.

I didn't say that. I think I said, "Maybe that clamp needs a lesson," and he got this look like I'd told him there was a sale on beer. He went and got his pistol. And bam, the clamp was history.

Oh, yeah, Tommy. When he showed up, my old man was in a shooting frenzy. It started with the clamp but went on to beer cans and me. Oh yeah, I was target practice. He'd never hit me. But it sure made him laugh to see me run.

Like I said, Tommy appeared. I know my dad didn't see him because he probably woulda shot him for trespassing. And then shot the dog for not barking. I was diving behind this refrigerator when I looked down past all the Chevy body parts and saw Tommy standing there with his goggles on. Then I heard the old man's gun jam. When I looked back, Tommy was gone and the old man was throwing the gun at my head. I ducked and kept running.

You know what's so fucking weird? Until that moment that

Tommy showed up—actually it kind of seems like a mirage now—I didn't know how fucked up the old man was. You know, you grow up and it all seems kinda normal. But having one person see what happens and it all looks sick. Like that was the first time I thought, man, my old man is one sick motherfucker.

I wish I knew where Tommy went. I'd guess I'd like to talk with him. As strange as he was, I still liked talking to him. He made me think about school differently. Like my old man thinks it's a waste of time. But seeing how smart Tommy was and the stuff he thought about, well, I don't know, I guess I wondered if maybe there was something I could learn that would, you know, help get me away from here.

Like I built a car, man. I'm not stupid, right? I mean, if I can build a car, I must know some stuff, right? Like maybe I could do good in school. I'm gonna be a junior next year. Maybe I could go to college.

So what are we gonna do? Drive around all night?

It's okay with me. That's what I do now. I go home after school and work for a while. Then I make the old man some food. Then I leave. I make up some excuse. School. Car parts. He's usually blasted. I go home after he's passed out.

It's weird. I think of Tommy when I'm sneaking back in. Like my old man's passed out in some other dimension and I'm stepping back into the one that he's left.

I also think about Tommy 'cause, with him being missing, I wonder if it's possible to find my mom. Like if we can find Tommy, maybe I can find her.

I swear I don't know where he is.

I know he believed all that shit he thought about. Who

knows? It could be true. I mean, if I can build a car out of spare parts on a shelf, who's to say Tommy hasn't stepped into another reality. I dream shit up to do with metal all the time. He dreams up stuff about time travel and alternate dimensions. If I dream shit up and make it real, why can't he dream shit up and make it real?

I mean, in my reality, he probably fell in a sinkhole. But in his reality? Who knows?

The Higgs boson is not the God particle.

First, it's confusing to mix religion and science.

Second, what the Higgs boson proves is the presence of the Higgs field, which causes particles to have mass. Scientists knew that particles had mass. What they didn't know was what caused those particles to have mass. They had a theory about the Higgs field, but until they found a particular boson with a particular weight, they couldn't prove the field existed. Now they do. Now we know how one particle achieved mass.

We did not find God.

McCloud says if we know what causes mass, then we might be able to figure out how much less mass is needed to move things through space. If we do that, then we can experiment with unlimited possibilities of propulsion. Like we might be able to reconceive transportation. Someday it might be ridiculous to drive a two-thousand-pound gas-powered hunk of steel to the store. Kind of like the way we look back and think that traveling by horse and buggy is old-fashioned.

I need to tell Alvin about the Higgs. He would get it.

THE COMIC BOOK

MARICELA HURRIES ALONG THE SIDE OF US 281 until she reaches the wide patch of dirt at the edge of the road. Even in the predawn darkness, she can see a few other workers. Some girls are sitting on the logs rolled under a bank of trees and bushes. Two of them hold lumps of children still asleep in their arms. A few men stand in the center, their heads topped with silhouettes of cowboy hats and gimme caps. Maricela looks for a space on one of the logs. She shuffles toward an opening, careful not to trip in the potholes.

Taking off her small pack, Maricela stuffs it under her legs and sits. Today's ride is supposed to be a couple of hours. Then they'll work. Then they'll find someplace to sleep. Then they'll do it again the next day and the next day. Once all the fields are planted, they circle back and pick them clean.

Maricela has been planting and picking for four seasons. Before that, she traveled with her parents and stayed out of their way while they worked. Every time she moves, she wishes she could stay a little longer in one place.

A pickup roars by and then screeches to a stop on the highway. Two more workers hop out of the back. One of them trips and swears. *"Chinga."* The other one laughs. Maricela recognizes Alfredo, the one who tripped. Both of them are loud, and the way their boots kick the rocks, almost tripping over them, Maricela can tell they are drunk. Some of the younger men drink all night to stay awake for the truck and then sleep until the next field. The pickup accelerates down the highway and the smell of exhaust drifts over everyone like dust. Then there is silence. All of them are listening for the sound of the vehicle that will take them away from this waiting place.

Maricela watches the horizon. She is waiting for dawn to crack the edge so she can read the comic book she found under the mattress in the trailer where she slept last night. She loves comic books. Especially the romantic ones. This one looks like an action comic with a masked figure on the front. Maricela imagines it belonged to a boy. He must have left it behind. Maybe as a gift. Or maybe he is hoping it will be there when he comes back. Maybe when she finishes it, she'll leave it behind in another trailer for someone like her. Maybe. Now she wants the sun to rise so she can read the pictures and figure out some of the English words.

"Chicle. Chicle." Juany's boy is whining for gum. As usual, Juany is ignoring him. Without looking, Maricela knows that Juany is fixed on Alfredo, while her little boy is searching her pockets for something to eat. Niño. That's all Juany's ever called him. She still hasn't given him a name. At least not one that

Maricela has ever heard. Always, Juany is looking at Alfredo. Especially after he has been drinking all night. Always, she wants to make sure Alfredo's eyes are on her.

Maricela glances at Alfredo, standing in the middle of the pull-out. In the dim light, Maricela can see Alfredo is not looking at Juany. Or their boy. He is staring directly at her.

Maricela sucks her breath in and bends over the comic book. If Juany sees her looking back at Alfredo, she'll come over and slap her. Not Alfredo. The look would be Maricela's fault. Maricela would be the whore, *la puta*.

That's how it is with Juany. Alfredo is her man ever since she went with him. No one else can have him and if anyone looks at him, Juany calls *her* every kind of whore. So the girls ignore Alfredo. At least when Juany is looking. When she isn't, all the girls sneak looks at him. As soon as they do, Alfredo catches their eyes with his and lingers on them. It doesn't matter if he is hunched over a plate of food or talking with the other men in the fields. Alfredo's deep brown eyes drift to the girl watching him and take in every inch of her. Without moving, Alfredo's eyes prowl after the girl. If she finishes picking one row of beans and turns to start the next row, Alfredo glances over at her no matter how far away he is and holds her in his gaze for a minute. Then he looks away. Only she still feels his eyes on her. The way a lizard might feel the paw print of the cat that pounces but lets him go.

Maricela has watched Alfredo do it dozens of times. Ever since he showed up in this area of Texas. Was it her first year, when she was eleven? Maricela scanned the calendar of seasons in her mind. Her parents got sent back last spring when she was fourteen. Juany had Alfredo's boy the spring before that. Juany went out with Alfredo three years ago but he came the spring before because she remembers Juany talking and talking about him.

Four years, she's been listening to the girls whisper about how he is *muy sexy*, how he looks older than their brothers but younger than their fathers. They sigh about him. Even the older women gossip about Alfredo. They talk about how his eyes creep down their skin like fingers. How could eyes be like fingers? Maricela didn't understand it. Now Alfredo's eyes are on her and she can feel them pulling her hair away from her neck, looking for any bit of skin.

Maricela doesn't look up. She can't. Not only because of Juany's temper. Juany's like a big sister to Maricela. Her parents told Maricela to stay in America where her birth certificate says she belongs. They asked Juany, three years older than Maricela, to watch out for her. Juany's helped her a lot, telling her when and where to show up for work, making sure Maricela has a place to sleep and showing her how to send money to her family. This past Saturday, she helped Maricela send money for Mother's Day. Juany doesn't ask for anything in return. Except she tells Maricela not to go with the boys too early. Especially not Alfredo. Especially after Juany got pregnant by him.

Juany went with Alfredo when she was almost sixteen. She told all the girls it would be different with her. He was her prize. She'd make him stay with her. She did, too. Not because he wanted to. She scared all the other girls away, calling them whores. Everyone knows that Juany is trying to hold on to Alfredo. No one would believe her if she called Maricela a whore.

But they wouldn't cross her either. Not Juany. She isn't afraid to pick a fight and make life harder for girls she doesn't like in the fields.

Maricela looks across the dirt expanse toward the highway. She wishes she heard the truck coming but all she can hear is Niño whining and coughing. He was up a lot last night, coughing and crying. It sounds like he is sick.

Bending forward so her hair curtains her face, Maricela peeks through the strands at Alfredo. She can't see his eyes but she knows they are looking for an opening, following her strands of hair past her neck, inside her blouse. *No lo mires. No lo mires.*

But she wants to look. She wants to know what eyes creeping across her skin feels like. She wants to hear his fingers tickle the screen of a trailer door and his voice whisper soft and coaxing, like his eyes, "*Maricelita, ven aquí.*"

Maricela had seen lots of girls tiptoe out the door to be with him. When Juany went out to him three years ago, Maricela found a sheet under the bushes in the morning. No one was on it. Only some reddish brown spots. It embarrassed Maricela. It was like they had left dirty underwear for everyone to see.

She stares at the comic book. The horizon has turned custard yellow and she can almost see the pictures. She pulls back the curtain of her hair and tucks it behind her ear. She doesn't look at Alfredo. But she knows his eyes are staring at her cheek, at the profile of her lips. She doesn't want it to excite her but—

Slap.

It sounds so loud in the early morning that, for a moment, Maricela thinks she's been slapped. When she looks, she sees Juany slapping Niño's arm. He is pulling up her shirt, trying to get at her breasts. Niño is screaming. Juany picks him up and walks over to Alfredo. She swears at him and hands Niño to him. She tells him to take care of his son and stop looking at Maricela. Maricela looks down. No one moves. Niño has stopped crying for the moment since he was in Juany's arms, but as soon as she turns her back he starts screaming again. Snot and tears are all over his face.

Maricela's eyes burn. She can see the white-faced figures in the comic now. One of them is wearing a mask and a cape. He is fighting a half-lizard, half-human creature. She can't read the words but Maricela knows that the half-human creature is evil because of the meanness twisted into the face of the drawing. It looks like Juany's face when Niño is trying to nurse and Alfredo turns away from her. It looks like the meanness of her wanting Alfredo to stay and hating how her boy hangs on her.

Maricela wishes she could fall into the squares on the page. Anywhere but here. She turns her head a little. Alfredo is still holding Niño like he is a sack of garbage that smells bad. Plus, Alfredo can hardly stand up straight, so he sits Niño on the ground next to him. Immediately, Niño pulls himself up on Alfredo's leg. He is still crying and coughing. Snot pools under his nose. His mouth is edged in dirt. His feet and legs are chalky with dust. Maricela wishes she had a cape and a mask. She wants to go over and take the boy away from Juany and Alfredo. She wants to stab Alfredo and take away the soft brown eyes that make all the girls want him. She wants to hit Juany. So hard she cries like her boy.

Maricela blinks. The page in front of her is blurry. One of the squares is bubbled and wet from her tears. Everyone in the pull-out has turned to stone waiting for the moment to pass. No one looks at the boy or Alfredo or Juany. Seconds slip by. The rumbling sound of a vehicle approaches. The girls on either side of Maricela stand.

Maricela wants to get up but she doesn't move. She wants to pick up the boy and walk out into the field beyond this stupid waiting place. She wants to show him the yellow flowers on the prickly pear cactus. They could pick one and blow the petals so they float in the air like butterfly wings. She thinks she remembers standing in a field with her father with butterflies all around them. Was it here or in Mexico?

A beat-up white van pulls to a stop at the edge of the pull-out. Maricela keeps her head down and doesn't move. Everyone else walks toward the vehicle. Alfredo picks up Niño and hands him to Juany. Immediately Niño stops crying. Alfredo weaves by Maricela, close enough so she can smell the sour odor of alcohol mixed with his cologne. Juany is right behind him. Maricela knows her feet. She's watched Juany paint her toenails and tell her how Alfredo kisses her feet and twirls his tongue around her ankle up to the inside of her thigh. She's made Alfredo's love sound so glorious. Like the kisses Maricela's seen at the end of the romantic comic books.

Maricela glances over at the van. Most everyone is on. Juany is about to step on when Niño starts coughing. He rubs his eyes and starts crying inconsolably. Maricela can hear the bus driver telling Juany she can't get on with a sick baby. Juany says he doesn't have a fever, only a little cough. The bus driver won't let her on. Alfredo is nowhere in sight. He is probably in the back of the van, passed out already.

The sound of Niño's crying gets louder. Maricela looks up and sees Juany standing in front of her with Niño on her hip, miserable. Juany looks at Maricela and she knows exactly what Juany is going to say. Juany has watched out for Maricela a whole year. She's not asked for any money from Maricela. What she wants is to be with Alfredo. She loves him. It may be wrong or stupid but she wants to be with him just like the girls in the romantic comic books want to be with their boyfriends.

Juany says all that with her eyes. Then she says, "*Me debes*," and hands Niño to Maricela.

Maricela takes Niño. She may or may not owe Juany, but if Maricela gets on that bus right now, Alfredo will put her on a crash course with Juany and the ending of that story would be bad for everyone.

Juany turns and walks away. Just as she is about to get in the van, she turns and calls to Maricela and says, "*Hasta pronto*." Then the van door slides closed behind her.

Maybe Juany is saying that so everyone will think she is coming back for Niño. Maybe she really means it. Maybe their paths will cross in some field, somewhere. Maybe next week. Or the week after. The trucks with workers go round and round through the fields and farms like the carousel Maricela saw in one of the towns where they stayed last year.

Niño wriggles off Maricela's lap and holds on to her knee, looking after Juany, but she has disappeared. The sunlight has cracked the edge of the horizon. As the light hits the bus, it blackens all the windows so Maricela and Niño can't see inside.

"Tilla?" The boy turns to Maricela, begging for a tortilla.

Maricela stares at him. His wet eyelashes outline his dark,

black eyes. He blinks at her as if he is trying to imitate Alfredo's winks. He has sweet eyes. Like Alfredo's. As soon as he could crawl, he begged tortillas from everyone in the camp with those eyes. The way Alfredo's eyes beg *besitos*, little kisses, from every girl he passes in the field. His eyes say he would die without those kisses. Like the boy's eyes say he will starve without those tortillas.

Maricela looks at the boy. His grubby hand is still on her knee, steadying his wobbly stand as they watch the van roll away. When they can't see or hear it anymore, silence floods the pull-out. The boy wobbles and falls. His diapered bottom plops onto the caliche. He looks up at Maricela. His eyes blink wide. His lower lip trembles. His face starts to crumple. Maricela reaches for him. As she does, she notices a small ring of keys on the ground. At first she thinks one of the other workers dropped them. But she didn't hear them fall and no one was standing in that exact spot. One of the keys has a black rubber top like a car key. Only it's small. Maricela wonders how the owner of the keys got home. Or if their car is stuck someplace else. She picks up the ring and fingers the three keys. Car. Home. What would the third one be? Maybe the home has two doors.

The boy reaches out for the keys but Maricela closes her fist around them and slips them in her pocket. She knows these keys aren't hers and the doors they open are invisible to her, but Maricela wants them. She wants them in her pocket. She wants to pretend she is the owner of the keys.

The boy grunts, stretching toward Maricela to be picked up. She pulls him onto her lap, wipes his nose, and opens the comic book. Together, they look at the pictures. Maricela studies one panel. The twisted half-lizard creature is on his back. His mean face looks in pain. Blood is leaking out his mouth. In the next panel, the man with the cape is scrambling up the side of the building to a little girl sitting on a window ledge. Behind her, flames consume her bed. Maricela tries to read the words in the bubble above the caped man's head. "Hold on. I am coming."

Maricela isn't sure what the words mean but it feels like a good thing might happen next.

I lost my notebook again.

Only I'm wondering if I even lost it. I went into McCloud's classroom about eight times looking for it. It wasn't there. I swear it. Then I go back in and there it is. How does that happen? I asked McCloud if it was possible for things to slip back and forth in the space-time continuum. He said no. Then he said what was more likely was I went into another dimension so my relationship to time and space and objects changed. So if I had the notebook in McCloud's classroom and then I left the classroom, only instead of leaving the classroom, I went into another dimension, I wouldn't be able to find that notebook until I came back to this dimension. So maybe I don't lose things. Maybe I go into another dimension. Maybe when I go into another dimension, I step outside time as I know it.

JAMES

THE LAST TIME I SAW TOMMY? TEN DAYS AGO. Friday. Physics class. It was the end of the day. He was sitting next to me doing his pencil-tapping, leg-jerking thing. He always did it at the end of class, when McCloud was droning on about due dates and the final. Tommy thought he could make time speed up. Like the force of his energy jerking in space would compress the minutes or make McCloud speed up. Drove me nuts. I'd point at my watch and tap it at the same speed as seconds ticking, like I was counteracting his energy force. Drove him nuts.

No idea where he was going. Tommy didn't do "See you later" or "I'm going to the Stillwell Ranch, wanna come?" He just went. The bell rang and he was gone.

Well, that's where they found his bike, right? Wait. Are you suspicious of me because I told you what everyone already knows? Whoa. Back off, Officer Krupke. I mean, Sheriff Caldwell.

Sorry, *West Side Story*. Musical theater reference. You probably wouldn't get it.

Tommy and I did not hang out. Yeah, I've known him since elementary school but Tommy didn't do hanging out. He was too intense. We've always been in the same science classes and he's always been my lab partner. Always. He's the only one who could keep up with me. Have you ever had a bad lab partner? They're really good at saying "Whoops, I forgot to keep the control clean." Or "I didn't chart the second step. Was I supposed to?" Bad lab partners are a pain. Tommy was meticulous. Obsessed. I loved that. But we weren't friends.

He's always been intense. Not in a sick way. Like he didn't catch bugs, deprive them of water, and chart their demise. It was more like when he was interested in something, that was all he could think about. Seriously. Pokémon cards when he was six. Daggers when he was ten. Genetics when he was fourteen. Particle physics now. He couldn't be normal about liking something. He had to collect every Pokémon card ever made. He had to draw every style of dagger since the beginning of time. He had to know every possibility of gene combination with recessive and dominant traits in order to figure out when blue eyes would show up in a predominantly brown-eyed family. Now he's obsessed with quantum. McCloud went off on a tangent about particle physics back in January and Tommy got all supernerd about the subatomic world and how the rules are completely different from the world we live in. It's kinda cool. How all possibilities exist until one is observed. But Tommy went off the charts about it. It was all he could think about. But that's how

Tommy is. It's like he goes into a different dimension when he's interested in something.

Girls? No way. Not interested. Yeah, of course he knew Rachel and Izzy. They're part of the famous nerd squad in our class. They've managed to keep up with Tommy and me in every AP science class. He might have even noticed they were girls. But as far as dating girls or being attracted to them or doing the whole mating ritual, no way. It's way too social sciences for Tommy. Too nebulous. Too gooey.

Rachel sort of acted like a mother hen with Tommy. Or like Miss Manners. Whenever Tommy would bolt at the end of class, she'd stop him in the doorway and ask him if he was leaving and he'd look up, down, and around like he was noticing where he was and then look at her like, well, I seem to be in the doorway and class is over so I must be leaving. He wouldn't say a thing. And she'd say, "Now is when you say goodbye, Tommy." And he'd say, "Bye," like he was parroting back some foreign language, and then he would disappear. Poof. Gone.

Personally, I think Rachel had a thing for Tommy. You know, a crush on him. She might have asked him to the prom. I think she wanted to. Or was going to. Before he disappeared. Me? No, I didn't go to prom. Let's just say the person I wanted to go with asked someone else.

No way. No one hated Tommy. I mean, he said inappropriate stuff, like one time this huge guy—his name is Robert—he wandered into our class by mistake and Tommy bumped into him or something. When he looked up at this huge guy, Tommy said, "You look like foreign matter." Everyone laughed. Even the big guy. That was Tommy. He said nerdy stuff like that. Nothing antagonistic.

Oh you heard about that? Yeah, I took some hits for that superior intelligence thing I wrote. I was calling it the way it already is. People don't like to admit it but they seek their own level. Like water. We think we are more inclusive but we're not. Cheerleaders are as narrow-minded as I am. I am just smart enough to admit it.

Tommy didn't have a group. He was random. I mean, you could say he was a science geek but he didn't really hang out in the lab or with any other geeks. He was in his own world.

Look, I'm smart, but Tommy's like expanded smart. His brain could wrap around all the possibilities. In all ten dimensions. He had the kind of brain that could handle simultaneous realities. Like most people have to prove that there is only one right answer or one right way to be. Not Tommy. That's why quantum physics and the superposition theory switched him on. If all possibilities exist, how does one right answer help us understand the problem? Does the problem still exist when we find the answer?

Like if you were asking Tommy where he was, he'd tell you he was riding his motorbike *and* walking across the field by the pull-out *and* looking for his notebook *and* going through a fold between dimensions *and* whatever else might be a possible reality. If we find out where he is, all the possibilities collapse into one observable reality. In a way, answers to problems are way less interesting than the problem.

I'm not upset, because I think he's out there. What? You think I'm not upset because I stashed him somewhere? What for? So he could give me the answers to the final? Yeah, right. I've known Tommy for a long time. He's out there. He wanders. He forgets where he is like he forgets his notebook, which is like his blankie. Most of us know not to loan him stuff because he'll get distracted and set it down and forget it. That's how he is. Maybe somehow he lost himself and he's landed where all our lost stuff is and he'll come wandering back with my Rubik's Cube from third grade and that set of superstrong magnifying lenses I had in sixth grade. Man, it was a pretty good thing he lost those. I was way too into making things spontaneously combust back then.

Yeah, I was there for every search. Actually it seemed like it was one big search for four days. I went out there a lot. The whole town was out there, walking side by side. I didn't think we'd find him. Like I said, I don't think he's dead.

Finding Tommy is going to be random. He was a random guy. That pull-out is a random place. I mean, it's a dirt patch on the side of the road but it's been there forever. People call it the Stillwell pull-out because it's been there as long as the ranch. Maybe longer. Someone started stopping there a long time ago and it kept happening. Why? Because the tectonic plates shifted in such a way that there was a hill on one side of the road and a field on the other? Because of the way the road curved around the hill and still left a big stretch of dirt? Because a couple of trees grew up around that dirt so people could stop to pee in privacy? Who knows? People started stopping there. To sleep. To sell shit. All kinds of people stop there. Tommy could have been snatched. He could have willingly gotten into someone's car because they asked him to. He's out there. Somewhere. We haven't figured where to look.

72% of leading physicists believe in some form of multiple universe theory.

They believe that the universe continually branches into countless parallel worlds. Whenever the universe is confronted by a choice of paths at the quantum level, it actually follows all the various possibilities. So if I think back to my beginning, when my mother gave me up for adoption, then there is another me who stayed with her, who is with her being raised by her. So right at the very beginning, I branched into parallel worlds.

Now it's more than two parallel worlds because everything I didn't do, every choice I didn't choose, is another wave of possibility that is me. I wonder if it's possible to rejoin those waves of possibility. Like if I went to meet my birth mother, would I rejoin the wave of me that started at the moment my parents took me home? I wonder if I become more by meeting up with the other wave that is me.

THE SMYTHES

MRS. SMYTHE: SHERIFF CALDWELL! WHAT ARE YOU doing here? Tom, the sheriff's here. Have you found Tommy? Have you heard something? Tom, hurry! He won't talk to me until you get here.

Well, at least you aren't interrogating us separately like you did before. That was awful, Sheriff. As if we did something to hurt our Tommy. I don't care if it's policy. You should apologize. Thank you.

Tom, what are you doing? Sheriff, can't you talk to me? He's up to his elbows in grease trying to fix an irrigation pump. He'll be in shortly.

Tell me, Sheriff. Has something happened?

You want to search his room again? What for? You have his computer. You've taken all his schoolbooks. There's nothing else in his room except his clothes. Did you want to take those?

Of course he had a library card. We could hardly keep him in books. Tommy was a very bright boy. Why do you need to see what he checked out of the library? This is ridiculous. How will that help you find him? How is looking at all the books he checked out of the library a possible lead?

Notes in the margin? Physics experiments he was interested in? What are you thinking? That Tommy did some experiment and disappeared? I can't believe you're listening to those kids.

Sheriff, you may look in every book in this house and in every library in Texas. But this so-called lead tells me you have no idea where he is. That's the real reason you're here, isn't it? To tell us there's no place else to look. That you're done.

Of course I'm crying. Our son is missing. If you give up, how are we going to find Tommy?

I know you don't have the resources to keep doing on-the-ground searches. I know the horseback search teams walked along Highway 281 for twenty-eight miles. I know we had over six hundred volunteers searching Hallie's ranch for four straight days. But, Sheriff, Tommy's still missing. We have to keep looking.

What about using dogs to search the ranch?

What about the FBI? Have they found anything?

What about—?

This is all our fault. We didn't contact you soon enough. We should have called on Friday afternoon. We should have made Tommy come right home after school every day. But, Sheriff, Tom said he needed his freedom. He said, "Tommy's sixteen. We need to loosen the reins." But we waited too long. I wanted to call at dinnertime when he wasn't home. But Tom thought maybe he was out with Rachel. He wanted to believe that Tommy was out having fun on Friday night. But Tommy didn't have a social life. He was shy. Awkward.

We should have called right away. I shouldn't have had a glass of wine at dinner. But Tom kept saying that Tommy would be away at college soon and we needed to get used to being a couple again. We never drink wine but we did that night. Tom cooked some steak and we had a nice dinner. I tried not to think about Tommy so I think I drank more wine than I should have. That's why I fell asleep. That's why we didn't call that night. That's why we can't find him now. We were too late.

But calling you at eight a.m. on Saturday morning is twelve hours after I should have called you. It's all our fault.

Do you realize we wouldn't even know where to start looking if that Travers boy hadn't found his motorbike in the pullout that morning? At least we know he was there on Friday afternoon after school. But there's been nothing else. Nothing from the Amber Alert. Nothing from the highway patrol. Nothing. All we've found on Hallie's land is a dump and a Mexican girl with a toddler.

It's not your fault, Eugene. It's ours, isn't it, Tom? Of course you're scraping the bottom of the barrel for leads. We called you too late. You can search whatever you want in our house. Excuse me. I need to get some water. Would you like some?

· · · · ·

Mr. Smythe: I think you understand, Sheriff, Tommy is our only son. Between the worry and guilt, it's more pain than she can bear.

So you really don't have any more leads? Did you check with the Gladney home in Dallas? And Tommy hasn't contacted them? I was hoping that would lead to something. It didn't seem like finding his biological parents was a burning desire but he was curious about it. Tommy could definitely be insistent if he wanted to know something.

Well, we didn't hide the adoption from him, if that's what you mean. Matilde wanted to wait until he was older. She was more sensitive than I was about not being able to have kids. She worried Tommy would want to run off and be with his biological parents if we told him too soon. Or that he'd run off to find them the first time we told him he couldn't do something. It was silly stuff but I kept quiet like she wanted me to.

It was a few years ago. As soon as he took that genetics elective in middle school, I knew it wouldn't be long. Sure enough. One Thanksgiving dinner with relatives from both sides of the family sitting there, Tommy figured it out. Mattie was bringing out the pie when he asked the whole table, "Am I adopted?" Dead silence. Mattie nearly dropped the pie. I said, "Yes, son. We met you when you were three hours old and if we could've gotten there sooner, we would have."

Well, you know that joke when the little boy asks his momma where do I come from and she thinks he's asking about the sex act so she's hemming and hawing about how to answer, and the little boy says, "Johnny says he's from Ohio so I was wondering where I came from." I could see Matilde tearing up over the pie as if Tommy might walk away from the dinner table because he was adopted and never come back. No one was saying a word. Then Tommy says, "I thought so because I'm the first Smythe to have blue eyes or a cleft chin. Those are both recessive gene traits." That was that.

Afterwards, we talked about the adoption some. Me and Tommy. Mattie didn't like talking about it. Tommy was curious about who his biological parents might be. But not in the way he could usually get about wanting to know something. He knew he had to wait until next year when he turned eighteen. He seemed fine about that. Ask Matilde.

. . . . .

Mrs. Smythe: Here's some water for you, Sheriff. Tom's right. I was the one who was the most sensitive about the adoption. Tommy was curious but not in the usual way he could be curious about things. He could get a little obsessed.

You know I called the Gladney Center for Adoption and told them what had happened. They said they hadn't been contacted by Tommy. They were very nice. They always treat adoptive parents like they are the real parents. They said Tommy's disappearance may not have anything to do with his being adopted.

Tom, the sheriff is here to tell us he has run out of leads and now he wants to look in the margins of books for Tommy.

I understand. Every time I walk outside, I look for Tommy. But instead of finding him, I feel like the world gets bigger. Like the possibilities of where he might be seem to grow and grow until I can't take another step.

A couple of days ago, I had an idea that maybe he walked out into Hallie's field and then he got hungry so he went cross-country over to the Whip In. So I did that exact walk. When I didn't find him, I wanted to turn around and try again but start in a different place and turn in a different place. But I could be one hundred feet off every try.

That's why we have to keep looking. Because he's somewhere out there and the world is a very big place. I know he's there. He's lost. He's hurt. But he's out there. You know when someone you love dies.

When my mother died a few years ago, I could feel it. She was in a nursing home in Fredericksburg. I was home. I was going to go visit her. It was after lunch, I remember, because I got up from the kitchen table and all I wanted to do was lie down. So I sat down in Tom's chair. I swear I could hardly keep my eyes open. I fell sound asleep for five minutes. When I opened my eyes, I knew she was gone. The phone rang and it was the nursing home, telling me she had died. But I knew before I picked up that phone. I felt it.

I don't feel the same way about Tommy. He's still here. Somewhere.

Please tell me you won't give up, Sheriff. Please tell me we can keep organizing searches on Hallie's land. He has to be out there. He'd go out there all the time. Even before we bought him that motorbike. He wasn't trying to run away. He was exploring. Hallie said she saw him out there a lot. Looking at things. Tommy could sit and look at things for a long time. After he got the bike, Hallie said he could still go out there as long as he didn't ride it into the field and scare the livestock.

He has to be out there. He stopped in that pull-out and went out to look at something. I know it. He took the key to the bike, for heaven's sake. He was coming back. Only something happened. Something happened and he can't get back to us.

I'm sorry, Sheriff. I know it doesn't help to cry but sometimes I just can't—I think I need to go lie down, Tom.

· · · · ·

Mr. Smythe: It's been like this for twelve days. She doesn't sleep. She drives up and down 281. She was up for hours on Tommy's computer until you took it. Now she goes to the library and uses the computer there. She says she's looking for clues but I think she's lost. Searching and lost at the same time.

She doesn't want to take any medicine. She doesn't want to go to sleep. She wants to find her boy. I can't say I blame her. Sometimes when I fall asleep, I forget it happened. It takes a minute or two to remember that Tommy's missing. I have to go through the shock and pain and worry all over again. Just to get to where I was before I fell asleep: hoping that we'll find him, hoping that someone will call, hoping that he's alive and safe.

I know. I know. Even Mattie knows. Tommy could have left the bike in the pull-out and someone picked him up there. He could be in Canada or Alaska. He could be long gone. But I think we would have gotten a hint about his wanting to run away. A map. Catching him on the phone with someone. E-mails. Heck, if he'd been running away, he would have taken his computer and some clothes. All he had was his school backpack. That's all. He wasn't running away. He wasn't—

But who would kidnap a boy and not call us or ask us for money or something? I can't think that people are mean enough to take a boy. I can't believe there's someone who wouldn't think he belonged to someone, someone who loved him and cared about him. I can't.

Mattie and I don't talk about it. Sometimes I'll look at her and I'll see this current between us. It's white hot and it's like we're seeing the worst possible thing that could happen to Tommy at the very same moment. It's like we're being electrified with fear. One of us will blink or the phone will ring and the current is broken. I swear I feel limp afterwards. Like I've been struck by lightning.

I never told Tommy that bad things could happen to him. I never lied to him. But I never told him about mean or sick people. Maybe I did him a disservice. It didn't seem like he could process that information.

Yes, I know Tommy's an unusual kid. The Smythes are simple folk and Tommy was pretty different. But what would a test tell us? If we had him tested and the test gave him a diagnosis like ADHD or autism or something else, what would we do different? He'd still be our really smart boy who didn't quite know how to hold a normal conversation. Matilde and I felt like every family has an eccentric cousin. Why not accept him the way he is and try to help him to get along in the world? Only I don't think I did. Sometimes I think about how Tommy annoyed so many people with his questions and literal answers. If someone didn't know him, they might get really angry with him. They might think he was being rude. I should have told him about the mean things in this world.

I heard Hallie Stillwell say she's thinking about taking that Mexican girl and her little boy into her home and I wonder if she should be that kind. I used to think that kindness saved the day but she could be inviting a whole cartel of trouble into her home. You don't know. I should have put more fear into Tommy. He was too trusting. Not cautious or scared enough.

You're welcome to take all the books in his room. The librarians in Johnson City and Fredericksburg were always getting books sent over from the university. What do you do when your son wants to talk with you about particle physics? Or string theory? One time he asked if I thought it was possible to get to another dimension without dying. I didn't know what to tell him. I don't know half the stuff he knows. I mean, I've heard of the big bang and black holes. Mostly from science-fiction books I read as a kid. Not from an AP physics class or books I checked out from the library. People around here, well, that kind of thinking is blasphemous.

Mattie and I are big on the truth. If someone asks a question, that means they're ready to hear the truth. But what do you say when someone asks you about possibilities, about things that aren't proven, that barely exist?

I told him what I thought was the truth. I told him that if you can imagine something, then it might possibly exist.

Now I wonder what he was imagining. I wonder what he was trying to find out.

McCloud said that a general rule among physicists is that if phenomena are not expressly forbidden, they are eventually found to occur.

Even though we can't get into a machine and travel backward in time, mathematicians have figured out equations that allow for backward time travel. We may not experience it yet but if the equation exists, so does the possibility.

HYPOTHESIS

"OOOPS, HANG ON, ALEX." IZZY BRAKES HARD AND turns her beat-up Toyota off the highway into the pull-out. The car drops off the lip of the highway and clunks onto the dirt and caliche. Izzy yanks the steering wheel left and right, trying to avoid the potholes, but with each turn the headlamps catch another hole right before the tire rolls into it.

"Whoa, Izzy. Slow down." Alex grabs the dashboard as the car rocks back and forth.

Izzy careens to a stop in front of a cluster of cedar and mesquite trees. A rusty old trash can stands in the way. She thinks about jumping out and moving it or knocking it over with her fender. Instead, she squeezes the car in between the can and the trees and parks as close as possible to the trees. The cedar branches scrape one side of her car. No biggie. She noses the car under the branches and looks in her rearview mirror. Perfect. Tucked under these trees with the trash can behind them, she hopes no cars passing by will spot them.

She turns to Alex. "Let's get out."

Alex doesn't move. "What the hell are we doing out here, Iz?"

"I want to talk."

"Why here?"

"Because I don't want to be in the library or your front porch where we usually talk."

"About what?"

Alex barely said a word the whole ride out here. Usually he likes hanging out and talking with her. Now he seems irritated.

"Come on, Al, let's get out of the car."

Alex doesn't say anything. He opens his door and stands beside it like he is obeying her order. "Okay. What do you want to talk about?"

"Geez, Alex. What'd I do to piss you off so bad?"

"As usual, you have no clue, do you, Iz?"

"What?" Izzy says, drawling the word into as many syllables as it took for her to toss her hair back and bat her eyes, trying to imitate a dimmer version of herself. She is hoping she'd get a laugh but, truth be told, she's a little mystified about why Alex is mad. It's not like he was doing anything except obsessing over typeface and font size.

"I'm in the middle of building someone's website. Yes, I know. Computer science isn't really science, according to you. But it's a job, by the way. It's nine o'clock on a school night during exam week. You come over to my house, stand in front of my computer, and order me to get in the car. You babble on about useless school shit instead of telling me what's going on. Now you are ordering me out of the car. You're bossy, Izzy, and it's pretty effing annoying."

"Oh." Izzy ducks under the trees and walks around to the front of the car. The heat from the car's engine seems to exhale onto her bare legs under her skirt. One of the things she loves about her longtime friendship with Alex is how he doesn't hold back when something bugs him; he tells her straight out. It makes it easy for her to cop to any mistakes. "You're totally right, Alex. I'm sorry. I had this idea and I wanted to tell you about it. You know, see what you thought. And I couldn't explain it while I was driving."

"Let me guess. Another hypothesis?"

Izzy can't see Alex's face very well but it sounds like he's smiling. "Yeah. Busted." She jumps onto the hood of the car and slides back toward the windshield. Izzy pats the hood, offering a seat to Alex but trying not to order him around.

Alex climbs up next to her. "Okay, so what is it this time?"

At least he doesn't sound mad anymore. Still, she wishes she hadn't jumped on the hood of the car so quickly. The way she'd pictured the experiment, they'd be sitting in the field on the other side of the pull-out where it was more private. If anyone stops here, which was a huge possibility since Tommy has only been missing two and a half weeks, they could be seen. But if she suggests moving, however unbossy, Alex might get annoyed all over again. She stares up at the twisted branches of the mesquite trees and into the black space beyond them. The sky is clear, with only a sliver of a moon hanging above the tree line. She reaches into her skirt pocket to make sure the small square packet is there. So the experiment won't be perfect. That's okay. She can still test her theory. Scientists are nothing if not adaptable.

"You know I went to the prom with Tim, right?"

"Yeah . . . how'd that work out for you?"

"Umm, well, it was interesting."

"Really? I thought you'd have to talk sports all night long."

"We did. I mean, he did." Izzy sighs. She'd always stayed outside the whole dating drama, but ever since she started tutoring in Darrow's regular physics class, she got to know all the squealy girls and jocky guys, people she never would have talked to before. When Tim asked her to the prom, it felt kinda cool and she thought maybe, as a junior, she should give it a try. So she did. Only Alex was right. Once they were outside of physics, where Izzy was the queen of ease and helpful answers, she didn't have much to say to this jock. And he didn't have a whole lot to say to her.

"Let me guess," said Alex. "You talked about the Spurs all night?"

"How did you know?"

"Rockets, Mavericks, Spurs. That's all those ballers talk about. I picked one team is all."

"Yeah, I learned a lot about the Spurs, all right."

She also learned a lot about what makes boys tick. All during the prom, Tim looked pretty awkward, like he didn't know whether to ask Izzy to dance or what to talk about. But if one of his teammates said hello, he smiled. If one of them said anything about the NBA conference play-offs, he looked excited. That's when Izzy figured out to ask him about basketball. As soon as she did, he relaxed. When Izzy didn't say much back and the conversation died, he started to look uncomfortable. It dawned on Izzy that maybe she was in charge of how the date was going to go. Sure enough, every time she asked a question about basketball, he got all talkative and happy. Izzy checked out her theory three times and every time it was true. As long as Izzy was willing to talk about basketball all night, even while they were dancing, they had a reasonably good time. Or at least they looked like a couple who were conversing and not staring in opposite directions.

Then Tim hung his arm around her neck and went silent. This new development happened as soon as they left the prom and were walking back to his truck. It puzzled Izzy. Somehow he felt comfortable enough to put his arm, which felt like a dead lab animal, on her shoulders, but he couldn't talk at the same time. Izzy dug up a stats-related question to see what would happen. Tim lifted his arm off her shoulder and started talking about free throws and percentages. Izzy nodded and listened until he stopped and then, plop. Arm on shoulder. What was going on? When they got to the truck, Izzy looked up and saw him glance at her, smile, and look away. An arena-sized LED banner scrolled across Izzy's brain: *He wants to kiss me.* Izzy looked up one more time. Tim glanced at her and looked away. She could see beads of sweat on his nose. That's when she knew she was responsible for the kiss, too. When Tim finally looked down, she gave him a kiss. Not a big one. Just lip to lip. But it sure changed things. All of sudden, Tim was smiling again. By the time they pulled up in front of her house, all Izzy had to do was look up and smile and then he kissed her. But she was in control of the talking, the looking up, and the kissing. It was like behavioral science.

"So what happened?" Alex asks.

"Not much. If I didn't ask questions about sports, we didn't talk."

"Figures."

Izzy hesitates a moment before she says, "I let him kiss me."

Alex doesn't say anything.

"It was okay." Izzy wishes she could see his face better so she could tell what he's thinking. She doesn't know whether or not to tell him about her hypothesis or just test it. As a scientist, she knows telling him would foul the experiment. But considering where she got the idea—the girls in pre-AP physics—maybe she should run it by him first.

"Are you still a virgin, Alex?"

"Umm, Izzy? Why are you asking?"

"Because I've been thinking a lot about the whole virginity thing."

"Huh?"

"You know, losing your virginity. Doing it with someone."

"Did you do it with Tim?"

Izzy laughs, surprised that Alex asked. "No way."

This conversation isn't going the way Izzy wants it to. Maybe Alex isn't as easy to manipulate as Tim. Maybe the blind approach is best.

"You like me, right, Alex?"

"Uhh, yeah."

"As a friend, right?"

"Yeah . . ."

"Have you ever thought about kissing me?"

"Umm, maybe. Sometimes. Yeah."

Izzy hesitates. Should she ask or not? "I was wondering if you would kiss me."

"What?"

Izzy can't believe it. Asking isn't working either. What is the problem? Izzy turns around on the hood of the car and faces Alex.

Alex sits up a little. "Here?"

"Yeah, here." Izzy leans into Alex and puts her lips on his. She presses into him a little. He doesn't budge. "Are you okay?"

"Iz, this is weird."

Izzy leans toward Alex again, not pressing against him but stopping a half a millimeter from his lips. This time, he kisses her back. His tongue touches the edges of her lips. Izzy smells peppermint soap on his skin. Or is it peppermint toothpaste? She opens her eyes. His are closed. She can't guess what he's thinking but from the way his tongue is working inside her mouth, he seems to be into the kiss. Izzy reaches over and puts her hand on top of the hard knot in the crotch of his pants. Alex flinches and stops kissing her.

"Izzy, what the hell?"

Izzy presses her lips into Alex's again and strokes him through his jeans.

"Geez, Iz." Alex relaxes back against the windshield. Izzy leans above him. As they kiss, she unbuttons his fly.

"Izzy . . ." Alex tries to sit up but Izzy keeps kissing him and reaches inside his jeans. Alex leans back again. He lifts his hips slightly and slides his pants down a little. Izzy wants to look and see the thing she is touching but Alex's tongue is deep inside her mouth. Tim's kiss hadn't felt like this. His tongue barely went past her teeth. Alex's tongue is probing and insistent. And soft. Izzy notices how Alex's penis is as hard as his tongue is soft.

Izzy lifts her skirt up and straddles him. Still kissing, she presses herself on top of him. On impulse, she kisses Alex's neck below his ear. She hears him groan a little and her name slip out in a kind of sigh. His back seems to arch as he pulls Izzy closer to him. For a split second, she wants to ask why kissing him in this exact spot makes all those things happen but she doesn't. Instead, she reaches between her legs. When she touches his penis again, it stiffens more, bucking a little in her hand. She hears Alex suck in his breath. *Is that good?* She doesn't know.

She also doesn't know how she is going to get the condom out of the pocket of her skirt and onto his penis. She hadn't anticipated how she would navigate this part. Putting a condom on seems like one big delay. Maybe she can put his penis inside her a little bit and that would count.

With one hand, she points his penis up between her legs. With her other hand, she moves the crotch of her underwear aside. This has to be like those tampon diagrams. She pushes herself down onto him, daring herself not to flinch even though it hurts and pinches all the way in. Alex isn't moving. Izzy sits up a little and tries to see Alex's face but the dim light from the moon is behind her and she is casting a darker shadow across him. She leans forward and tries to kiss him but his lips don't open. She raises her hips up and tries to move up and down but she can't. It hurts. This isn't going how she thought it would. Alex isn't into it like she thought he would be. His whole body seems kind of rigid. She doesn't know what to do. Alex is supposed to like doing it, the way Tim had liked kissing her. Maybe she should try kissing him again. He seemed to like that a minute ago. She leans toward him and tries to kiss his neck. He flinches and jerks away from her a little.

"Alex, I want to do it."

"Izzy, get off me."

"But, Al, let me explain."

"Izzy. Get. Off. Me."

His voice pushes her off him. As soon as Izzy sits on the hood of the car, Alex slides off and stands with his back to her. It looks like he is buttoning up his pants.

He's breathing hard. She doesn't know what to say. Saying something might make him walk away. What had gone wrong?

The girls she tutored made it sound like all guys want to do it. They said that as soon as you kissed a guy, he wanted to do it. That's why the girls were so stressed out about their virginity. If guys want to do it all the time, girls need to figure out when to lose it, who to lose it with, where to lose it, and what age is the right age. Losing one's virginity seemed like this nerve-wracking, big deal.

Which made her wonder, after her experiment with Tim, if she could control when she lost her virginity. What if she made it *not* such a huge deal? What if she did it with Alex, her best guy friend? It should have worked. If all guys want to do it, it should have worked. Only the way Alex reacted, it seemed like the experiment had gone way wrong.

She slides off the hood and stands next to Alex. "Al?" He doesn't look at her or say anything. At least he doesn't walk away.

"Alex, what's the matter?"

Silence.

"Alex, I'll apologize but you need to tell me what I did wrong."

"Jesus Christ, Izzy. You really don't know, do you?" Alex turns and faces her. Izzy can't read him. He sounds mad but the night shadows are mottling his face so it looks like a mask is covering it.

"No. I mean, I told you I wanted to do it."

"But I didn't!"

Alex's voice slaps Izzy. She can't think. Her brain is scrambling, trying to find the right answer. It feels like she flunked the final. She had that sick "I'm going to fail" feeling in her stomach.

"Izzy, replay that whole scene. Only this time, I'm forcing myself on *you*."

"But, Alex, I was trying to lose my virginity with my friend."

"What the hell?"

Alex's question gives Izzy an opening. "It was that date with Tim. He wanted to kiss me but he was nervous. So I kissed him and then he wasn't nervous. I thought I could do the same thing with my virginity. You know, not have it hanging over me. You know, like how people stress out about the right time and the right person and the right everything." Izzy can hear herself babbling. She sounds desperate. And stupid. As stupid as all those girls talking about their virginity.

"You wanted to lose your virginity so you'd be less nervous about having sex?"

It sounds so selfish the way Alex says it. That isn't how she meant it. It's like he's sneering at her. More than anything, she wants him to understand. "I thought if I lost my virginity in a controlled environment with my friend, then I would be less nervous and be able to make a clearer decision when I wanted to make love with someone else. In the future." Izzy wills herself to keep standing there. She knows her friend Alex would think about this hypothesis. But this person standing in front of her doesn't sound like Alex. He sounds mean and angry. He sounds like someone who doesn't like her.

"So you fucked me to lose your virginity." His voice is sharp. It echoes in the silence.

"But that's not what I . . ." Izzy fumbles, trying to find the words that will explain.

"That's not what you meant?"

Izzy can hear the sarcasm in Alex's voice. She wants to get her friend Alex back. "I'm sorry, Alex. I thought that you would want to."

"Because I'm a guy? Because my dick is erect? Geezus, Iz, for being one of the smartest girls at Fred High, you are really stupid."

"Ouch."

"Oh, I'm sorry. Did that hurt you?"

"Alex . . . please . . ."

"What, Iz? What do you want now? You want me to understand your hypothesis and be okay with it? You want to discuss it? Do you want to call me after you made love to some guy and tell me the results of your hypothesis? You know, you can let me know if you were less nervous the second time. Oh wait, you won't need to, because now I can have sex without worrying about losing *my* virginity."

Izzy had never heard Alex sound this mad. Every word felt

like a push. A slap. Usually their arguments were competitions, like who was better at computer games (Alex) or logic puzzles (Izzy) or sports (neither). Izzy couldn't remember a time when one of them wasn't elbowing the other to share something mind-blowingly cool or gross or stupid. They'd had one awkward time in middle school when Alex said he had a crush on someone but wouldn't tell her who. Izzy remembered she got so mad at being kept in the dark that she didn't speak to him for weeks. Somehow, they started talking again. Izzy couldn't remember how. She never asked him who he had a crush on. She was just glad the fight was over and they could be friends again.

In a way, Izzy feels that same mad, desperate feeling she felt in middle school when Alex wouldn't tell her what she wanted to know. He is so stubborn sometimes. Why can't he understand what she is trying to do? It had all been so simple when she'd thought of it. Nervousness before a first kiss? Get it over with and then the next kiss isn't such a big deal. Worried about your virginity? Have sex with a friend so the whole virginity issue isn't a factor when you decide to have sex with someone. Maybe she set it up wrong. She wants to turn him around and explain it again to him. But touching him, even his arm, seems like a really bad idea. She knows better than to defend herself. That will make him madder. All she can do is stand there and take it.

"I'm sorry, Alex. Maybe I should have changed the experiment so that you knew what I was trying to prove. Maybe I should have factored you in."

"Ya think? Or maybe you shouldn't have done it."

Alex's words make Izzy back up onto the hood of the car.

Now what? She'd explained. She'd apologized. She'd said she did the experiment wrong. There was nothing else on the checklist of fixing a problem.

"Where did I go wrong, Alex?"

He turns away from her.

"Please. I don't understand."

Izzy thinks she hears him sigh. She isn't sure if it's an irritated sigh or a ready-to-give-in sigh.

"Iz, you're *supposed* to feel nervous when you kiss someone."

Izzy feels a "but" ready to pop out of her mouth. She stops it from coming out.

"You're supposed to feel out of control when you let someone kiss you. And then you're supposed to let go and trust that person."

It's like she's in a class where the teacher is explaining something for the fifth time and everyone else understands but her. "I don't get it."

Alex turns and faces her. "You really don't, do you?"

"No." Izzy hates admitting that. She likes being in the driver's seat. She likes feeling like she figured it all out. She doesn't like standing in front of Alex feeling more exposed than she was on the hood of her car. "Explain it to me again."

Alex leans down and kisses her. His arms reach behind her. She feels him pull her up and into him. His lips are soft. Izzy can't keep from wondering why he is kissing her, when he stops. She knows the kiss is meant to be the explanation but she doesn't get it.

Izzy looks up at Alex. His fingers thread her hair and then trace the side of her face. His smile reminds her of how Tim looked at her. But that isn't who Alex is to her, right? She wants to land someplace certain. That's how she likes her life to be. But right now, the only certainty is that she is standing in the Stillwell pull-out, about twelve miles outside of town. That's it. She isn't sure Alex is her friend anymore. "Please. Explain it to me again."

"I can't, Iz."

"But everything can be explained."

"Maybe. Maybe even this can. But I don't want to map it out with charts and graphs for you. I like the nervous feelings. I like feeling tipped upside down inside when I'm kissing someone special." Alex shrugs his shoulders like he doesn't care if he convinces her. Then he turns and walks in between a cedar and a mesquite tree at the edge of the pull-out.

The way Alex disappears makes Izzy think of Tommy. How he used to vanish at the end of class. How he was gone one day and now no one can find him. A lot of kids at school are saying that because no one had found his body, Tommy must have figured out a way to step into another dimension. Izzy wonders if going into another dimension looks like Alex walking through those trees. Is that really possible? Of course, it's possible. If you can lose a best guy friend in one night, anything is possible.

Izzy can't see Alex. She listens for his footsteps in the pasture beyond. She wants to go after him. She wants to explain her theory again. She wants it to make sense to him like it does to her. She wants him to say, "Oh, that's what you meant. Now I get it." But it doesn't feel like that's going to happen.

The wind sifts through the branches. At first, Izzy only smells the mesquite's tangy sweet smell. Then she smells peppermint. She looks around. "Alex?" But she's alone.

Again, the smell of peppermint. It must be on her skin. From Alex kissing her. Izzy can feel the way his lips press against her and pull her into him at the same time. She feels herself wanting to drift into the feeling of the kiss, but then she wonders how it's possible to push against someone and pull him into you at the same time.

She feels the fizz of a new idea bubble inside her.

Maybe she's stumbled upon a mathematical equation that no one has ever thought of. Or some energy force that hasn't been calibrated.

She wants to go tell Alex. She wants to see his face looking down at her.

Maybe this is what he was talking about. Maybe his kiss had tipped her upside down. Just a little.

Before being observed, the system takes on all possibilities. So reality is created by the observer.

But what if there isn't an observer? Reality is still going on, right? If I'm walking in a field, I exist, don't I? There are things out there that are observing me as existing. There are bugs I'm stepping on. There are animals smelling me. Is that enough to create a reality?

But what if there is absolutely no observer? Then anything is possible. Anything. I could be anywhere. I could be dead. I could be sleeping. I could be on Ruby going to class. I could even be in class because that's one of the possibilities that exists as long as no one is observing me.

So who is the observer? Who makes reality real? And do I exist if no one or nothing is observing me?

RACHEL

I DON'T HAVE ANYTHING DIFFERENT TO TELL YOU since Tommy first disappeared. He walked out of physics class almost three weeks ago. As soon as the bell rang. It wasn't unusual. Even if he had no place to go, he always got up and left when the bell rang. It was like the end of a book. You close it. You go. That's the way Tommy was. I mean, is.

Yes, of course, I think he's still out there. I have to believe that. Don't you? Isn't that why you're interviewing me again?

I usually asked Tommy where he was going, but that day he was already out the door before I could. I didn't always get a straight answer even when I asked. I mean, sometimes if I asked Tommy what he was doing, he'd say, "Talking to you." He'd say exactly what he was doing right then. I had to be specific because he was very literal. Like I had to ask "Where are you *going*?" or "What are you *going* to do?"

Yes, of course it could be frustrating. It's frustrating I didn't ask. It's frustrating he never said. It's really frustrating that you're asking me questions I've already answered.

Wait a minute. Are you trying out some sort of theory that I was somehow mad at Tommy and I knew where he was going and I followed him like a jealous girlfriend and something happened? That's unbelievable. I need to go.

I've come out to the pull-out every day since we first knew Tommy was gone. I keep expecting he'll be here. That he'll show up like the way he walked into class with his head down, like he was late. Only he never was.

James is an egomaniacal idiot who only wanted good grades and a good lab partner. I wasn't trying to improve Tommy's manners. Or be his surrogate mother. Or be his girlfriend. I mean, I liked him. And yeah, I was thinking about asking him to the prom, but it probably would have been a really bad idea.

Tommy was, I mean is, really different. He's this really smart but really innocent guy. Izzy and I had a theory that maybe he had Asperger's. Ever since I knew him, the beginning of high school, he was always fixated on something. You couldn't shake him loose. When he was like that, he'd barge into any conversation with whatever he was thinking about. He didn't know when to say "excuse me." He wasn't aware of normal stuff. So I started helping him, you know, with social cues. I cared about how people treated him.

It wasn't manners. James is the one who needs manners. Tommy needed help knowing how to be in the world. I guess I feel protective of him. He was really smart but it's like he needed help crossing the street.

Of course I'm mad at James. He sat next to Tommy for three years. He made sure Tommy was his partner on every project. He could have asked Tommy where he was going. Or something. If James said one little thing to Tommy at the end of class that day, maybe I could have gotten over to Tommy before he left and asked him where he was going. Maybe I would have gone with him.

He got the bike sometime last fall. One day I asked him for a ride home. I remember how he looked behind at the seat. I could almost see the thought bubble over his head, "Oh that's why the seat is longer than a regular bike seat." That was one of the things I loved about Tommy. The simplest things stumped him.

I didn't "love" love him.

Wait. Izzy told you I was his girlfriend? Figures. Izzy's obsessed. A total mad scientist compared to Tommy. Tommy would wait and watch before he tested a theory. Not Izzy. She'd fling theories all over the place to see what stuck.

That whole boy-girl thing—pretty much the way high school is set up—it doesn't compute that way for Tommy. I don't even know if I was his friend. Like his brain is so different, I don't know where I lived in it. Or if I did. No, that's wrong. I *was* his friend. He always smiled when I went up to him and said hello. I just couldn't expect him to come up to me and say hello.

I don't think his awkwardness made him depressed. He didn't know he was awkward. He was Tommy. We're the ones that thought he was awkward.

No, no one bullied him. I would have seen it.

Wait, if you're thinking he committed suicide, you're crazy. He was way too curious. Quantum was blowing his mind. It's pretty deep stuff. I hung in there with him but he was off the map about it.

All of it. Superposition theory. Alternate dimension. Time travel. Black holes. He was—well, this might sound strange—he acted like someone who was in love. You know that first crush? When all you can do is think about that person and write poetry to them? That's where Tommy was with particle physics. It's all he could think about.

That's what is scary to me. When he was like that, he was so wrapped in what he was thinking that he wouldn't pay attention to what was going on around him. Like he might have been standing in this stupid pull-out staring at something or thinking something and someone drove in and grabbed him. You know, like a random act. And then because that person didn't know Tommy and how he answered questions in the most annoying ways, that person might get mad. And Tommy wouldn't understand why that person was mad and he'd say something which would frustrate that person even more and—

I'm sorry, Sheriff. I get scared for Tommy. Most of the time, I'm hopeful but sometimes I'm scared.

He believed anything he could think was possible. If it wasn't proved but he could think it, then it was just a matter of time before someone proved it was real. He believed that simultaneous realities were possible. He believed that everything had energy and you could communicate with that energy. That was why I liked being with him. He didn't think in confined, "normal" ways. Being with Tommy was like a free fall.

I rode on the back of Ruby maybe a half dozen times. Maybe

more. It was like being inside his brain. He'd go crazy fast and then he'd stop practically in the middle of the road and watch these flocks of birds dip and turn through the air currents. They looked like smoke to me. I don't know what they looked like to Tommy. I mean, we never said stuff like, "Oh, that's beautiful." Or "Oh, that looks like smoke." Looking at the birds together in the same moment was the conversation. I mean, if you're with a guy who is thinking that each person, each thing contains waves of possibilities and those possibilities might exist in alternate dimensions, then you can kind of see how being together seeing the same thing at the same time is a pretty big deal. That's how Tommy thinks.

Yeah, he figured out he was adopted in middle school. It's kind of weird his parents didn't tell him. I mean, they have this genius living under their roof. How long did they think it would take for him to figure out that he's got a few recessive traits that aren't in their gene pool?

I know he was curious about his bio family. But it's not like it was new information and he was all hot to find them right now. If he had to wait until he was eighteen or twenty-one, it didn't matter. Besides, he didn't really want to meet his bio parents. He was more interested in meeting up with a former self. I remember he said something like, "I wonder if I'll also meet the part of me that stayed with them." Like when his parents adopted him, a part of Tommy kept living on with his bio family. That's how he sees stuff. Like we're all waves of possibility and whenever we make a choice, part of us energetically continues going in the path not taken.

I don't know if I believe it. It's kind of cool. But it's almost a little too much. Too theoretical. I like more concrete science stuff like biology or chemistry. Physics is too unreal. It has too many possibilities. It makes me kind of crazy. Like I said before, it feels like a free fall, and sometimes that gets a little scary.

Tommy was fearless. I mean, is.

It's what made him Tommy. He was never afraid of any of the possibilities he thought up. If time could fold in such a way that he could go backwards, that was okay. Exciting, even. He wasn't scared that something bad could happen. Being afraid was as weird to him as saying "excuse me" or "goodbye." I don't know if he felt afraid ever. I mean, he probably did because that's normal, right? But he was so observational that understanding a feeling made more sense to him than feeling it.

When he left class really fast and didn't say goodbye, I told him it made me sad. He didn't get it. I showed him a definition of *sad* in the dictionary. Then I made the mistake of giving him an example of people being sad at funerals. Metaphors were lost on him. I remember he said something about the probability of his coming back to school the next day is a hundred percent because he's never missed a day of school. Do you see what I mean? He didn't feel feelings the way we do. Sometimes I wished he did because then he'd know how the rest of us felt. But at the same time, that's why I wanted to protect him, because I didn't want anything bad to ever happen to him. So he would keep being innocent. And fearless.

Yeah, I know I freaked out that first day of searches at the Stillwell Ranch. It was too much for me. I kept feeling like Tommy was there. Like he was right next to me. Only I couldn't see him. And then when we got to that ravine with all the trash, it looked like this graveyard where all the possibilities in life had come to die. Like the minute before we saw all those refrigerators and tires and old suitcases, they were still out there, existing the way they always had been. But because we saw them in that dead, decomposing state, all the possibilities collapsed. It freaked me out. That's why I didn't go back on the second or third day. It was too hard to walk and hope and walk and hope. The whole time I was dreading what we might find. I know we didn't find Tommy or his body, so he could still be out there, but hope will make you as crazy as particle physics. I want to stop hoping. I want to stop looking. But I also want to keep hoping and looking because that means Tommy's still out there.

That's why I come here. It's my way of looking. Sometimes I sit in my car. Sometimes I get out and sit on one of those logs and listen. Sometimes I walk around in the field.

I see Mrs. Smythe out there. She looks like she hasn't slept in three weeks. Tommy wouldn't want to be driving her crazy with fear and hope. He might even understand it by looking at her face.

You know if Tommy were here right now, I'd have to explain to him about hope. He wouldn't understand. There's observation and possibility. But hope? I could try and explain it like when you have a hypothesis and you want it to turn out a certain way, that desire would be hope. But it wouldn't compute for Tommy. I can hear him asking me, "Why would you want something to turn out a certain way?"

Do you see what I mean? It's like all the normal emotions—hope, fear, sadness, anger . . . Tommy doesn't really get them the way we do, on an experiential level. If he did, he would come back. He'd know how we were feeling and he'd come back from wherever he is. At the same time, it would be awful if he were in a situation so terrifying it short-circuited his brain. Like completely fried his wiring.

I'm sorry, Sheriff. I really care about Tommy.

He's out there. I know it. He's missing. It's like this bright, really bright, pure spot of light is missing. And I want it to come back.

Maybe that's how I could tell him about sadness. I could tell him about a beautiful light that he'd seen every day. Every day he woke up and it was there. He expected it. Looked forward to it. And then one day it was gone. He might be able to understand being sad if I explained it like that.

Observation of a rabbit:

Every time it stopped to eat, its ears twitched. Then its nose twitched. It was eating to survive. And it was using all its senses to stay alive. I must have been downwind. It didn't smell me. It hopped closer and closer. I could hear the crunch of the leaves in its teeth. Then the wind shifted. Or I moved. It took off. A trail of pellets behind it. Rachel would say the rabbit was afraid and ran. I don't think fear exists for animals. I think they smell and hear and react. That's all. We name it fear. I'm not sure it's fear. It's how they survive. But is it fear? I don't know.

MR. McCLOUD

TOMMY WAS THE BRIGHTEST STUDENT I'VE EVER had. I have to say teaching advanced physics to the junior nerd squad was the highlight of my year. Kids like that make teaching a little harder. Better but harder.

Because you want to spend all your time with them and you can't. You have to help everyone. I teach almost three hundred students a year here. From freshmen to seniors. As much as I would have liked to spend all my time doing special projects with the nerd squad, this is high school and I have to teach to the middle. That means you leave the smart kids and slow kids in the margin.

It's tragic. It's also why I stay. Because I love public education. It doesn't always work right. And certainly all these standards and tests do not serve the kids, but this job is still the best way for me to reach the greatest number of kids and maybe help them see that their minds could make a difference.

I'm sorry, Sheriff. You didn't come here to listen to my soapbox on teaching. You want to talk about Tommy.

First of all, don't believe any of the bull crap the kids are saying about Tommy going into another dimension. Not possible. Yeah, Tommy was a freak about quantum. No question. But as for the space-time continuum folding over in some specific way so that Tommy was able to cross over to another time, no way. It's fun to think about and I love conjecturing about all the possibilities with these kids, but we are not living in the panels of Marvel comics.

Yeah, I took a week in January to talk about modern physics. You know, particle physics. Just concepts; no math. It was outside the curriculum. I like doing it because it gives students an idea of what's possible in college. Not all of them liked it or understood it. Tommy did. I've never had a kid get as switched on about it as Tommy. I gave him a bibliography of books and secondary resources to check out from the library. If he wanted to learn about quantum mechanics, there's plenty out there. He could have spent an entire semester doing an independent study on any one of the quantum principles, like superposition, but I had to go back to the curriculum.

One of the ideas that Tommy loved in quantum is that all possibilities exist. Nothing is certain unless you include every possibility. Believe me, we had a lot of fun with that one. I gave them a quiz and Tommy turned his in blank. Not one answer and it wasn't because he didn't know the answers. When I asked him why, he said if I hadn't observed him *not* doing it, then the possibility existed that he did do it. I hated to give him a zero, but the blank test was the only reality I observed.

Black holes? Time travel? We never talked about those aspects in class but I'm sure he read about it. I know he wrote about them in his journal. He was always writing in it. Or looking for it so he could write in it. That's why I gave him a bibliography instead of books. He had trouble hanging on to things.

I read bits of it. Mostly he was wrestling with the big ideas in physics and conjecturing about our origins. Writers love those ideas. And I don't mean science-fiction or TV writers. Academics explore these topics as much as novelists. You don't have to go far to have your mind effectively blown by quantum theory. It's rocket fuel for the brain and the imagination and some high school kids like Tommy are ready for it.

Dangerous? Hell, no. Not any more so than that motorbike, if you ask me. A kid like Tommy, highly distractible and driving, now that's dangerous. I was glad that they found the bike in the pull-out. If Tommy was still out there driving around, we'd probably be looking at a traffic fatality.

I wouldn't be surprised if Tommy was somewhere on the spectrum. But he functioned pretty well. He was socially awkward but the kids seemed to accept him the way he was. I don't think it would have made a difference if he were diagnosed. I think that leads to stigmatizing. When it's all said and done, spectrum kids still have to function in this world. We can't create separate little paradigms for each quirky kid.

Especially in high school. This is the time when these kids start making choices that define them. Like the nerd squad probably won't be the nerd squad next year. Their science interests are starting to diverge. Like Tommy's friend Rachel will probably go towards anatomy and physiology or AP bio; Izzy has more talent in math and equations, so I'll probably see her in AP physics C, and James is on the pre-med track, so he'll take AP chemistry. I hope he stays on the lab side. I can't see him tending to patients.

Tommy? Who knows? He was one of those kids who had to endure high school to get to the good stuff. For some, high school is the highlight of their lives. That wasn't Tommy. I could see him in a university with professors who appreciate really smart kids. Some kids take longer to come to a boil. You know, flourish. Go places. That was Tommy. I was glad he took to quantum. If anything, it gave a kid like him something exciting to think about.

Well, let's face it, Sheriff. Tommy was sort of an outlier in the Fred Johnson High social test-tube experiment. He didn't exactly fit in the categories of farmer, football player, or family man. These kids come in and out of our classes day after day and you know who's going to get pregnant. Or who's going to go to college. Or who's going to stay on the farm. Some of 'em surprise you, but not many. I think we're genetically predetermined. Like each of these kids is an element with certain properties and they'll only go so far because that element reacts in predetermined ways.

Hell no, I'm not being dismal. It's the way it is. I mean, some of these kids may find themselves in unusual circumstances. They may get torqued in such a way that their properties change. Experiments can turn strange corners, you know. Some kids break out of their predetermined fate. But not many. Not many of us change our destinies or step out of our well-worn paths. If people accepted this idea, they might be a whole lot happier. I mean, someone has to wait on you at the Home Depot. Why can't it be someone who's happy about it? Why can't it be someone who's accepted the fact that that's who they are, that's as high as they'll go?

No way. I did not preach this idea to my students. James came up with that line of thinking all by himself. What's more, I don't agree with it. James is very smart, but his whole elitism ethic is a way for him to camouflage himself. Well, let's just say that this neck of the high desert is a little conservative and it's easier for James to come off like an IQ Nazi than what he is. That's all I can say. Sorry.

As a teacher, you're outside the day-to-day drama. If you're paying attention, you know your kids better than they know themselves. You know when someone has a crush and if they are going to act on it. You know who is getting beat at home. You can see turf wars. You see flirtations. You see kids hiding their true feelings. I used to get worried about all the things I saw. I may not be a parent but I still feel protective of these kids. I thought I had to do something about it. You know, intervene. Tell the counselors. But it took me one four-year cycle to see that everyone survives. Everyone. There are ups and downs, crises and triumphs. But everyone survives in one way or another. Maybe you want more for these kids than survival. But after you've been doing this for twenty years, survival is not so bad.

Besides, being different isn't a bad thing. Like I said, Tommy was really brilliant. I couldn't tell what elements or compounds he was made of, but he was really smart. I thought he'd find his way eventually, but he hadn't come to a boil yet. Like he had undeveloped properties. Maybe ones that haven't been discovered. I'm probably pushing this analogy too far. Scientists can be poets, you know. Or philosophers.

Past tense? I didn't realize I was. I guess it's habit. It's the end of school. I always use the past tense with my students when school's done. I think we're all looking in the rearview mirror by the end of May. Like I said. Habit. I assure you I have no knowledge of Tommy's whereabouts and I did not see him in the pull-out when I drove home. If I had, I might have stopped. You know, asked him what he was doing. Maybe told him to watch out.

Let me show you something. Tommy wrote this in the margin of the last test he took in my class. He got done early, I guess. I keep holding on to it even though school's over for the year. It seemed like something he would want to put in his journal.

When a bell rings, it affects each of us differently. It may make me leave class. It may cause an animal to run. It may stun an insect. Who knows how it affects a flower? All of these realities are true. And real. And they all exist at the very same time the bell rings. So why not parallel universes?

I want to believe he's out there. I want to be able to give this to him. Three weeks is a long time not to have any clues. I drive by that pull-out every day, back and forth to work. There's always someone stopped there. As smart as he was, Tommy was pretty innocent. Some drifter could have approached him. Who knows? One question—even "What's your name?"—can turn in a thousand different directions.

Most scientists agree the universe is expanding, and as it expands, energy fields called black holes get created to take up that negative space. Scientists also agree that black holes swallow light and mass and they may signal the end of our universe.

But according to the law of conservation of energy, the total energy of an isolated system cannot change. Energy can be neither created nor destroyed. It doesn't end but it can change form. Like from chemical energy to kinetic energy.

Here's the thing about black holes. They have energy that creates particle pairs. The energy from the black hole pulls the pair of photons apart. One of the pair goes into the black hole; the other goes in the universe. So the universe, or rather the energy of the universe, is always creating life, going towards life, even in the midst of an energy that could swallow all of life.

Maybe when we die there is a part of us energetically that keeps living, just like that photon on the edge of a black hole.

LOST

KARLA STANDS IN THE MIDDLE OF THE PULL-OUT. The pickax in her hand is sticky with blood and brain and hair. She hears the gurgle in the man's throat and then silence. Just her own breath. Hot and sharp. In and out.

She rubs her face. It's wet. Sweat stings her eyes. How could she be hot? Isn't it nighttime? She looks up to find the full moon that had been hanging above her windshield all night long but it has fallen. Almost to the tree line.

On the ground near her feet is a patch of white. At first it looks like a bit of the moon's shadow through the trees. But it's too bright. Karla reaches for it. She wasn't expecting to pick up a sheet of notebook paper. She thought it would be a napkin that had blown out of someone's car. Or some other bit of trash. Karla turns it over and sees a few lines of handwriting.

Need to tell Alvin that I named my bike Ruby. He said it had to be a girl's name and match its personality. I don't think a bike can have a personality. But I found a name that matches the color. And it's a girl's name. I looked it up. Yeah. Ruby.

Karla turns the paper over hoping there's something else on the other side. She wants to know more about Alvin and Ruby and whoever wrote this funny little note to himself. Or herself. It seems like the stupidest and most important note in the world. She wishes that she had written it. She wishes she knew an Alvin. She wishes she had a bike with a name she'd chosen.

She looks around. Has she been to this pull-out before? Its semicircular shape looks familiar. Or is it a different one? It has to be different. She's miles from Texas City. Miles from the pull-outs there. Miles from the bars and honky-tonks and the long flat stretches of highway cutting through the marshes. Where is she? What time is it? This time of night always confuses her. Is it late? Or is it so early the sun isn't up? It's like the compass of time doesn't work in these blank hours. Always Karla feels unmoored, like she's drifting and lost.

· · · · ·

Her momma always woke Karla up at this time of night. Sometimes with yelling. Sometimes with giggling. Always with the smell of cigarette smoke drifting over her like a gauzy blanket.

This time, her momma was giggling. Karla lifted her head off the belly of the stuffed bear she used for a pillow and peeked over the edge of the front seat. Cigarette smoke curled around her momma's thick, dark hair. She was staring straight ahead and laughing. Karla could see a pair of red lights, like eyes, staring back at her momma. The tip of her momma's cigarette flared as the car surged faster. Karla felt the speed press in on her stomach. The car shifted and jerked her body across the backseat of the car. The plastic upholstery was cold in the new places she touched. It woke her up more.

"I'll get you, you S.O.B.," her momma yelled out her window. The giggle was gone. She was on the hunt.

Karla reached for the stuffed bear and pulled it to her. "Momma—"

"Shut up, Karla Ray. I got to get our money. That S.O.B. thinks he's gonna get a free one offa me, he's got another thing coming."

Karla felt the car accelerate again. Her momma honked the horn. The blasts whipped by the open windows. Karla peeked out and saw the edge of a dark pickup loom alongside. A man in a white cowboy hat was framed in the window. He was laughing. In his teeth was a bill. He took it out of his mouth and held it outside his car like he was going to drop it.

The car swerved. Karla slid across the backseat. Her momma held the wheel with one hand and reached across the seat with the other, trying to grab the bill.

"Goddamnit. Jimmy, stop your goddamn truck and pay me my money."

The pickup truck slowed but it didn't stop. The man reached farther out the window. The bill flapped in his fingertips.

"Karla Ray! Get your little butt up and get my twenty bucks."

"But Momma—"

"Get it before I stop the car and beat your backside twenty times."

Karla set her bear on the floor and knelt on the backseat. She leaned out the window and grabbed onto the handle above the door. As she stood, she leaned farther out away from the car. The man's hand was right there. She could grab the bill and be done. But the hot wind caught her. It whipped through her hair and across her face. The stink of the heavy marsh air was gone. It was warm. She reached past the man's arm and hung her body farther out the window. Maybe she could fly.

Slap. Her thigh burned.

"Karla. Quit fooling."

Karla pulled herself back inside the car. As she did, she grabbed the bill out of the man's hand and flopped onto the backseat.

The white of her momma's palm flashed in front of her face. "Give it."

Karla handed the bill to her momma and picked up her bear.

"That's a good girl."

The two vehicles were still barreling down the two-lane blacktop. Karla looked over at the man in the pickup truck. He was staring at her. Then he leaned out the window, slowing down a little.

"How much for a poke at her, Sandy?"

"Way more than twenty bucks."

"How much for another one with you?"

"Depends on what you want."

"Same. I'm a married man."

"Pull over."

Karla felt the car slow down and bump as the tires dropped off the highway. Then it jerked to a stop. The gravel and sand skidded to silence. As soon as they stopped, the oily marsh air crawled in the window and lay on top of Karla. The night glowed orange with the refinery lights across the marsh.

The front door opened and slammed shut. Karla watched as her momma strutted up to the man walking toward her. She only came up to his chest.

"You better pay me first. Goddamnit."

"You're a tough little bitch."

"That's right. Just the way you like me."

Her momma's palm flashed again. This time at the man. He pulled out his wallet and put a bill in her hand. She walked to the marsh side of the man's truck but the man didn't move. He was looking into the car at Karla. Karla wasn't sure he could see her so she hugged her bear in front of her and slid farther down in the seat to make sure he couldn't.

"Let's do it right here."

Karla's momma turned. She was standing off to the side. Karla could see her face framed in the passenger window. She followed the man's eyes to the backseat where her eight-year-old daughter sat. At first, anger flickered in her eyes and her mouth tensed like it always did when Karla sassed her. Then Karla watched her momma's lips curl like another car chase had started and she was going to win.

"Having an audience'll cost extra."

"How much?"

Karla watched her momma measure the man, trying to figure out how much extra he'd pay, how much would drive him away. "Another twenty."

He pulled out another bill and handed it to her momma. He never stopped staring into the car. Karla saw her momma step toward the man. She took the money and dropped out of view. Karla heard the gritty notches of the man's zipper. She slid down in the backseat till all she could see was the blank starless night. She knew the man was still looking in the car. She heard his hands grab the hood. She could feel the car rock in time with his grunts. Faster.

It was almost over.

It had just begun.

. . . . .

"We'll make it like a party, Karla Ray. It will be a party," her momma said. "A thousand-dollar party. All paid up. We'll give you a little hoochie hooch, make sure you're nice and relaxed. Then you lay there and let him do his thing." Her momma was standing in front of the bathroom mirror putting on makeup. Karla Ray perched on the back of the toilet and looked at herself in the mirror. In some ways she looked like a carbon copy of her momma. Full crazy-curly hair, brown eyes, short and thin body. But her momma looked like a woman. Karla thought she looked like a boy with boobs.

"What if he doesn't like me, Momma?"

"Oh, he'll like you. Believe me," she said, pulling Karla off her perch. "You got a nice tight little body. Your boobs have perked up. Besides, you don't have to be good, he paid a thousand dollars for a puredee thirteen-year-old virgin. That'll be excitement enough for George."

Karla's momma crooked her finger under Karla's chin and looked in her eyes. "I'm so proud of you, honey. This money's gonna help us out. With two of us earning, we can really go places. We might be able to get our apartment back." She smiled at Karla and kissed her cheek.

Karla was happy to be helping her momma. That part was good. Even the thought of moving back into an apartment made her glad. She didn't like living out of their car or always having to check out of motels by noon. But sometimes the men scared her. She'd heard all their grunts and groans. She'd heard the names they called her momma. She didn't like the way they glared at her. Part of her wanted to crawl on the floor of the closet with a pillow like always and let her momma take care of the men.

"I'm not sure I can do it."

"Of course you can, honey bun." Her momma put her arm around Karla's shoulder. "This is like your first day at a new job. It's normal to be nervous. Remember, he's the boss, and if you do what he says, everything is going to be fine." She poured some clear liquid from a bottle. "Drink a little vodka. It will help you relax."

The liquor burned in Karla Ray's mouth. Her throat closed. She choked.

"Probably shoulda mixed it with some juice for you but we don't have any. That's right. Get it all down."

Karla gagged but swallowed all of it. She felt it burn in her stomach. The Happy Meal her momma still ordered for her because it was cheaper came hurtling up. She leaned over the toilet and puked.

"Better here than in the bed," said her momma. "Now brush your teeth and we'll have another little drinkie."

Her momma poured two glasses half-full of alcohol. As Karla spit out the toothpaste and rinsed her brush, her momma sprinkled some perfume on the back of her neck. It was from the little special bottle that her momma always kept at the bottom of her purse.

"The men like it when you smell good. One of 'em told me one time that it made him think I was his own private flower. Isn't that nice?" Her momma handed her a glass. "Let's hope you find someone who wants to make you his flower."

"Like get married?"

"Sure. Or take real good care of you. You know, set you up in style. Now let's have a toast. Tonight's the night you are going to become a woman and I am so proud of you."

They clinked glasses. Karla's momma drank hers in three gulps. Karla sipped hers.

"Keep drinking it, honey. It's for your own good."

Karla grimaced and swallowed again and again until it was gone. She felt her stomach want to pitch it out but she made herself hold it down. She'd taken sips of her momma's drinks before and they'd never made her sick. Everything about this night made her feel sick.

"That's right. Let it tingle all around. Feel better?"

Karla nodded. She didn't but she knew what her momma

wanted to hear. After a few minutes, it felt like the alcohol by-passed her stomach and went straight to her head.

"Good girl. Now you do what he says and you'll do fine. Besides, you've listened to me take care of the men enough times, you'll be a natural." She checked her watch. "It's time. Let's go."

Her momma opened the bathroom door just as there was a loud knock on the motel room door. She grinned at Karla, excited. "He's here. Your first one is here, baby."

Karla tried to smile but she felt a little wobbly.

Her momma opened the door, giggling and purring. "Don't you look handsome, George. Oh Karla, look at your date. George, I think you know Karla."

The man was wearing a black cowboy hat, a black shirt, and pressed jeans and boots. A toothpick stuck out the side of his mouth as he grinned at Karla.

"Now you be good to my little girl. I'm going down to the lounge and see if I can scare up a little business myself."

Karla's stomach lurched again. Her momma had said she'd stay right outside the door. She gulped some air so she wouldn't puke.

"There's some liquor in the bathroom, George. She might need a little drinkie and I promised her a party." And then her momma stepped through the door and was gone.

"Oh, we'll have a party, won't we, little girl?" the man said, sliding the chain lock across the door. Then he turned to Karla and unbuttoned his shirt. "I'll be here all night and you got a thousand dollars worth of party to give me. Now pour me a drink and get into your birthday suit. I got some cherries to pop."

· · · · ·

The thousand dollars didn't take Karla and her momma any-place new. Her momma did get them a cheap apartment off I-45. She even enrolled Karla in a middle school and turned tricks all day long at the apartment while Karla was in school. Until a neighbor complained. Her momma said it was because she didn't give it to him for free. Either way, they had to move to a by-the-week motel. Her momma said she made a deal with the manager, which included cheaper rent as long as she did her business (except with him) off the premises. Karla tried to keep going to school, but because her momma needed help with the men at night, Karla couldn't wake up early enough to get to school. She didn't really mind. She liked being with her momma. She liked helping with the men sometimes. What she liked best of all was when they got back to their room late at night and she and her momma sat up talking. Her momma usu-ally poured them a drink and lighted cigarettes for both of them. They'd laugh about the men, how all of them complained about their wives not giving them any. To Karla, it seemed like the secret to staying married was giving your husband a blowjob once a week. Karla would listen to how her momma would give certain men time limits if they were too drunk to get a hard-on. Always she told Karla, get the money first. "They get all sleepy and forgetful after they get their rocks off." These were the times Karla felt closest to her momma, like they were sis-ters. Sometimes she told Karla about the nicer men, the men who were regulars and slipped her extra money. Karla knew her momma hoped they would come back for her. Take care of her. After she talked about those men, she usually fell asleep with a smile on her face.

In the morning, though, her momma was grouchy with a hangover. The twenties didn't seem so plentiful and the round of bars and kneeling in toilet stalls or outside on gravel loomed closer. For three years, Karla and her momma worked the dance halls and lounges up and down I-45 from Houston to Galveston. At the dance halls, her momma would go in the front door, because she was over twenty-one. By the time she got to the back door to let Karla in, her momma had six tricks ready for Karla to turn. She'd march Karla right to the men's room and tell her to get to work. When she complained, her momma would say, "We've got to make a hundred and eighty dollars tonight. How do you want to do that?"

One time Karla suggested she get a job dancing at a topless bar. Her momma shot that idea down. "First of all, men only put dollars in that G-string, not twenties. So you might wag your butt around that bar all night and only make twenty bucks. Besides, you have to be eighteen to work there. You'd probably make a lot more money turning tricks outside the topless bar than dancing in one." More and more, her momma was less like a sister or a friend and more like a boss.

They stayed at motels farther off the highway, sometimes driving all night to find cheap ones. Her momma taught Karla to drive in case she'd had too much to drink or they needed to drive longer than she could stay awake. The next night, they'd head back toward the dance halls and lounges and bars, looking for cowboys. Her momma was always looking for cowboys. She thought they had more money. Karla knew she secretly hoped she'd find a rich one. Karla doubted it would ever happen. She felt like those cowboys probably treated their horses better than they treated her or her momma.

One night, when Karla was seventeen, she pointed to a biker bar off the highway. "Let's hit that one."

Her momma shook her head. "I don't like bikers."

"What's the matter with bikers?"

"They're mean."

Karla laughed. A short, sharp laugh. The kind that might double as a slap across the face. The kind that shoved the other person away. Karla yanked the car off the highway and cut hard across the access road into the parking lot of the bar, which was filled mostly with Harleys. Karla opened the car door and got out.

"Where the hell do you think you're going?"

"You can have your ass-slapping, butt-fucking cowboys, Momma. I'll take my chances with the mean bikers."

Karla slammed the car door and walked toward the bar. She felt a little wobbly. It was the first time Karla had ever stood up to her momma and did something different. She heard gravel crunch under the tires. She was sure her momma had slid across into the driver's seat and was pulling into a parking space. But then she heard the car accelerate and the gravel spray as the wheels sped out of the parking lot. Karla almost stopped to look back. If she had, she might have seen the chasm of air that her momma left behind. She might have felt that sudden emptiness press on her heart. She might have stopped and run after the car and her momma, yelling. But she didn't. She knew her momma wasn't turning around either. She imagined her momma's eyes were squinted like when she got mad. She was probably lighting a cigarette and blowing the smoke out hard. Karla paused a second or two at the sound of her momma's departure. Maybe one footfall took a little longer to hit the ground. But she kept going.

When Karla walked into that bar, she stopped being a hooker or a prostitute or a little bitch, piece-of-trash whore. When Karla walked into that bar, she became a party girl. By the end of the night, she became Russ's party girl. By the next day, she was his girl for keeps. He brought her back to the house he said he shared with two other guys, Sean and Tad. It was a big house with more bedrooms than people to sleep in them. It looked like a mansion with a wall all the way around it and a pool in the backyard. He told her Sean and Tad were his business partners. They didn't look a thing like cowboys. Russ wore a bandana around his head with aviator sunglasses. His beard was shaggy, and when he laughed his belly jiggled. Karla couldn't tell how old Russ was. Maybe forty. Sean and Tad were skinnier versions of Russ. Definitely younger. None of them looked as old or as mean as the cowboys she met with her momma.

Russ told her he would take care of her if she'd be his girl. He gave her pills to help her stay up all night. He slipped hundred-dollar bills in her jean pockets so she had some spending money. Sometimes Russ and his business partners had parties for their customers at their house. That's when all the bedrooms got used. Sometimes Russ asked Karla to have sex with his customers as a favor to him. He didn't make her do it. He asked her if it was all right first. Sometimes he stayed in the bedroom, watching her do it. He said it was to make sure she was safe. When it was over, he told her she did real good and then he had sex with her. He kissed her. He closed the bedroom door so he could do it with her all alone. Then he slept with her. Karla had never slept with a man before. Sometimes he kissed her before they went to sleep. Karla had never been kissed that way before. All these "never befores" made her feel special. Sure, she didn't like it when he paid attention to other women, but he told her that was normal, the way he let some men pay attention to her. She was still his girl.

For four weeks, Karla climbed on the back of Russ's sleek black Harley and wrapped her arms around his belly. She loved pressing into the back of him and smelling the salty sweat on his neck. Sometimes she thought she could smell some kind of perfume on his skin. It reminded her of the soaps in the motels where she and her momma stayed. She didn't like it.

Every once in a while she'd see her momma's car parked in front of one of the cowboy bars. She wanted to stop and introduce her momma to Russ. She'd landed in a way better place than her momma. Karla had a place to live, and every day was a party with Russ. She was going to make it. Who knows? Maybe she and Russ would settle down. It could happen. Maybe she'd ask him to stop and meet Momma next time.

Only it never happened. Six weeks after Karla walked into that biker bar, Russ left. He took off when Karla was still asleep. She woke up with Tad crawling on top of her. She pushed him away.

"Get off me. You need to ask Russ first."

"I don't need to ask Russ shit. He left you to me."

Karla felt an ice-cold current shoot through her. It jerked her out of bed. It kicked Tad to the floor.

"What do you mean he left?" she yelled. "He couldn't leave. I was going to be his old lady."

"You ain't shit," said Tad, gasping and holding his stomach. "He's got an old lady and a kid and a farm past Austin. He comes here to make sure our product is clean. You know, quality control. When he goes back home, I get his leftovers." Tad tried to get up. Karla kicked him again and again, until he stopped moving, and then she stomped out of the room.

She ran to the other end of the house and slammed into Sean's room.

"Where's Russ?"

"Holy crap, Karla." Sean rolled over. "Knock first."

"Where the fuck is Russ?"

"His farm. He's gone. He might be back in six months. Maybe a year."

Karla glanced around the room. Sean had gigantic pictures of mountains all over his walls. In between two peaks hung a small pickax. She grabbed it.

"Hey, what the fuck? Put that back."

Karla leapt on top of Sean and swung the pickax so it pierced clean through the pillow into the mattress.

"Next time, it won't be next to your head. Where is he *exactly*?"

"Some town outside Johnson City. Off Highway 281. West of Austin. His number's in my cell. Jesus Christ, Karla."

Karla looked at the bedside table and grabbed Sean's wallet, cell, the keys to his truck and a baggy full of white, green, and black pills.

"Hey, that's my—"

Karla stood on his chest and leaned the top, flat end of the pickax against his throat. She put her weight against it. Sean choked.

"I'm taking your goddamn truck, Sean. And if you stop me, I'll kill you."

Sean didn't move. He watched Karla empty his wallet of cash and stuff it and the cell phone in her pocket. Then she fished two black beauties out of the baggy, popped them in her mouth, and took a swallow of the leftover rum and Coke by the bed. She walked out of the room with the pickax slung over one shoulder and the bag of pills in her hand.

· · · · ·

Karla didn't let herself think as she drove.

With each pill, Karla could hear her heart race faster. She could hear her blood *thrum, thrum, thrum* by her ears. It focused her, kept her alert, made her keep pressing the gas pedal so she could get to Russ. The thrumming sounded like Russ. As long as she could keep that sound in her head, she would make it. She didn't want to think. She didn't want to stop.

But she had to stop twice. For gas. Stopping meant thinking about something other than Russ. Stopping meant going to the public restroom. Stopping meant thinking about all those bathroom stalls, all those men with their pants unzipped. She bought another Coke and swallowed five white crosses from Sean's baggie of pills. She had to get that thrumming back. She had to get Russ back in her head. She had to stop thinking about the men and Momma. She had to stop wondering where her momma was and what her momma would do.

For five hours, Karla drove like this. Popping pills, drinking Coke, and listening to the thrum of Russ. When she pressed his name on Sean's cell phone, it was after midnight. She heard his sleepy voice and almost hung up. She could imagine that he was sleeping next to her and she almost didn't want to disturb him. But then she thought of the woman next to him. "I'm in a fucking pull-out. I passed some ranch called Stillwell about a mile back. If you don't meet me I'm going to fucking come to your house and kill you and your fucking family." She heard him say he was coming and hung up.

Karla paced in the pull-out. She took another pill. The thrumming had changed to *he's coming, he's coming, he's coming, he's coming.* She squatted and peed. For the first time, she noticed that the hot sticky marsh air was gone. She'd never been anywhere but up and down I-45. She didn't know that there was a whole world different from the one she'd grown up in. She guessed that some of the men they met came from different places, but her momma told her not to ask. "Don't chitchat, Karla Ray. If you do, they'll start asking questions like how old are you and why aren't you in school? You don't need to be in school. You're smart enough as it is."

Karla shook her head. She stood up and paced around the truck. Then up and down the pull-out. She didn't want to think about her momma or the men. She wanted to think about Russ.

He's coming. He's coming. He's coming. She was going to get him back. She was going to make sure he loved her, that he never let her go.

When Russ finally drove into that pull-out, Karla wasn't sure it was him at first. He wasn't on his beautiful Harley. He was driving a stupid pickup like all those cowboys. When he stepped out of the cab, he looked old like all the other men. Where was the Russ she'd fallen in love with? How did he get so old all of a sudden?

All the miles of driving, all the liquor and pills were pacing inside Karla. She roared into him. She was mad that he'd changed. She wanted him to be the man she'd fallen in love with. She wanted him to take care of her. She tried to pull him into her with her arms, her legs, her mouth. He kept pulling away from her. He untangled her arms from around his neck and held her so she couldn't move. Each time she tried to squirm away, he said things like "best I ever had" and "I wish I could but" and "I can come see you in six months." Karla knew he didn't mean any of it. She knew he wasn't any different from any of the men who'd been her customers. She stopped squirming. He let go of her and turned to walk back to his truck. Like all the men who had zipped up their pants and turned away from her. They boiled inside her. She thought Russ was different. She wanted him to be different. But he wasn't. She wanted everything about her life to be different. But it wasn't.

Karla reached into the pickup for the ax.

Matter seems to be solid but it is composed of protons, electrons, and neutrons. And the gaps between these subatomic particles.

Everything is composed of particles that have spaces between them. Even us. We're made up of solids, liquids, and gas. And the space between those atoms and molecules.

I think it is the spaces between the particles that link us together. The spaces allow for us to be interconnected. If we were completely solid, we wouldn't be alive. The spaces between make us alive and allow us to connect.

It reminds me of how Mary Louise paints green in her paintings. She puts a lot of different colors in the green like she's painting all the bits that make up green. Even the spaces in between.

Particles. I think that's all we are. And the spaces in between.

MARY LOUISE

TOMMY WATCHED ME PAINT.

When he first came into the art room—I think it was in January—he didn't see me in the back until I started cleaning up. He looked really startled. Really. You know that expression "deer in headlights"? That was his face. I got a little worried, like maybe he would stop breathing from being on the spot, so I told him to chill. Like it's cool to hang out in the art room. I went there at least two lunches a week to work on my pieces for the senior art show. I invited him to come back anytime. That's where I'd see him. In the art room. Writing in his journal. Or reading some complicated science book.

He was so cute. I pointed him out to Leann one time. She called him "adorkable."

At first he sat way on the other side of the room, but one day he sat, not closer exactly, but so he could see what I was painting. I caught him looking over at the canvas so I asked him what he could see. It was a landscape and he said, "Trees." Then he said, "Eyes." I swear I did not put eyes in that painting, so I asked where he saw the eyes and he said, "In the spaces between."

That's when we started having these long, trippy conversations about art and truth and beauty. Only he came from this science-y place and I came from this art-philosophy place. But the two aren't very different. I swear if they taught science the way he thought about it, I probably would have liked it. Maybe gotten a better-than-passing grade.

Well, we talked about whether or not the trees I painted were real. Like if there were no trees in the world, would the trees I was painting be real? Would I have the thought about trees if there were none in the world? Or would I imagine them, and if I imagined them, would a tree start existing out in the world because I thought it? He made me think a lot about what I *wasn't* painting, what I *couldn't* see, what *might* exist if I could see it.

The eyes? You mean like was he paranoid? Like maybe he thought someone was after him? I don't think so. It didn't seem like he was hiding out or looking over his shoulder or like someone was out to get him. I think the eyes were his eyes. Like he was an observer. Like he could see all the spaces in between. Or maybe it was he could see all the connections in between. Yeah. That seems more like it. Because of how he talked about physics.

Well, okay, I'm not like a science girl, okay? So I'll probably get this all wrong, but he explained how matter looks solid but it isn't. There's like space between all the particles, right? So, like, even the most solid-looking thing has space in it. Like even you and me, there's space in our cells and our blood and yet we're one thing.

I think that's how Tommy sees the world: all connected together even though there's like a bunch of space in between and inside each thing. It's so cool. It made me think about how people love falling in love, how they're trying to fill up the spaces inside themselves and feel connected in the world. You know?

He made me think about God. How if a god made this world, then of course that god would design it with spaces in between, because when we feel connected to art or to another human, that's when we feel God. We never actually talked about God, but that's sort of what particle physics sounded like to me. God and the origin of things.

Did Tommy have a girlfriend? Uh, I doubt it. I mean, I saw Rachel get on the back of his bike a couple of times. They looked really cute together. But they could have been going off to do a science experiment. For real. He seemed pretty innocent to me.

Like he was supersmart but not in a real-world kind of way. He would get tripped up in simple conversation. When I'd leave the art room and I'd say something like, "See you next time," instead of saying, "Okay," he'd say, "What next time?" It's like he had to be superliteral about everything because he was thinking in so many different dimensions. So if I said something casual or unspecific, it caused like static in his brain and he had to stop and tune the channel.

Yeah, I've heard people saying that the reason we haven't found him is because he's in another dimension. I'm not sure that's possible, but if it was, it would be so cool.

Because it would be like he's still alive. It's been a really long time since Tommy disappeared, right? Yeah, six weeks. If Tommy's dead, we can't see him anymore. Everything he was in this life stops. But if he's in another dimension, it's like he's alive. I know I'll remember my conversations with Tommy for the rest of my life. Like the way we talked expanded me somehow. If he's dead, those conversations are a memory. If he's in another dimension, it's like that conversation could still continue. Like maybe he could come back from another dimension, only he'd be the same age as now and I'd be older because time is different wherever he went. Maybe that's why he was such a stickler about time.

I've probably got all this time-dimension stuff wrong. But I wonder what Tommy would say about that guy getting killed in the pull-out. Like did his life really end? I mean, Tara and her mom had her dad's body cremated afterwards, so it seems like he's dead. But what about that whole other life he had down near Houston, is that part of his life still going on because those people don't know he's dead? It's weird, right?

Maybe people are saying Tommy went into another dimension because they don't want to face the fact he might be dead. But death might not be so bad. One time he looked at one of my landscapes and said, "Do you think there are dead things in there?" Trippy, right? So I said, "In my painting, no. In the forest. Yes." I wanted to be very definite. Because, as I said, he was very literal. Anyway, he said something like death is a different state of being. When I asked him what he meant, he said, "Death is happening all around us. It's not an end. It's another way of being."

It's true, isn't it? Like right here at Little Creatures Daycare, there are probably organisms alive in my yogurt while I'm eating it. Who knows how many bugs the kids stepped on when we went outside for a nature walk this morning? And that outdoor faucet where we wash our hands after art? See how that water drips on those rocks? I know for a fact that green moldy stuff is alive and well down there and who knows what's growing or drowning under it. Life. Death. They walk hand in hand.

I probably sound like I don't care. I do. I went out to the Stillwell property and did every walk after he went missing. I'd go again if you had another search.

I look for Tommy all the time. Last week, I saw some of those buzzard-looking birds circling a field and I stopped my car. I walked maybe a half-mile into the field to see if it might be Tommy's body. It wasn't. It was a dead deer.

I felt funny walking into the field. I half wanted it to be Tommy so we could stop wondering where he is and I half didn't because I want to keep hoping that he'll come back. Knowing he's dead, if that's what's happened, would be a relief for his parents so they can stop wondering and worrying and looking. But knowing would be so final.

One time there was this fly in the art room. It was buzzing and buzzing and bumping into the windows. It was driving me nuts. So I opened the window and kind of whacked at it to push it out the window, only I whacked at it too hard and it died. I felt kinda bad but Tommy said, "Don't worry. In another reality, it's still alive."

You know, I bet that's why he was so awkward with casual conversation. He was always thinking of another reality.

Oh, no way. You stopped at my house and my mom showed

you my paintings? She wasn't so sure about me being an artist but when I got accepted at some pretty big-deal art schools and Parsons offered me a lot of assistance, she stopped being worried for me and now she can't stop showing off my paintings. I'm going to leave at the beginning of August. My whole family is driving me up. That's why I decided to stay and work at Little Creatures this summer. Once I go to New York, I don't know when I will be back.

Oh cool, you noticed them. Yeah, I started putting eyes in my paintings. Not in an obvious way. But subtly, so Tommy would know they were my paintings. Like someday, when my paintings sell all over the world, Tommy might be in someone's home or maybe a gallery or a museum and he'd see a painting of mine with the eyes staring out at him and he'd remember back to this past year and he'd look to see if I was the artist. And when he knew it was me, it'd be like time traveling.

Rachel asked me today if I think about her. I said yes. She said how? There isn't a how. How means there's a methodology in the way I think of her. I don't have a methodology. I mean, I know what methodology is. I use it when James and I do experiments. Methodologies are an orderly way of examining something in a lab setting. It's a controlled way of testing a hypothesis.

Why would I have a methodology about Rachel? When she jumps on the back of my bike, I think, "Rachel is coming with me." She doesn't ask where I'm going or what I am going to do. She gets on and we go. I drive differently when she is on the back of Ruby. Is that what she means by "how"? I mean, I have to accelerate differently around the corners when she's on the back. But that's a different method of driving.

I did notice the color of her hair. Some people would call it brown. But that's not descriptive enough. It looked like the color of this sand on the Stillwell Ranch. In the spring, there's a creek in the far northeast corner of the property. It takes a long time to get there because I can't ride Ruby.

It must be spring-fed because the water comes up out of nowhere. It can't be nowhere. It has to come from somewhere. I should explore that someday. Where the spring comes from. Yeah. That would be something to do someday. Anyway, there's some sand. Right where this water comes up, it's red and golden. It looks brown like her hair. But if you look closely there's all these colors in the brown. Yellow, white, black, red . . .

I didn't know the answer to Rachel's question but I kept standing there because I liked looking at her hair.

WATERMELONS

JAKE PULLS HIS TRUCK DEEP INTO THE NORTHWEST corner of the pull-out, angling it so the bed faces out to the highway but the cab is shaded by the only half-decent-sized live oak in this dirt patch. Slowly, he unlatches the tailgate, careful not to let any of the fifty or so watermelons he has piled up in the back come tumbling out. Once the gate is down and none of the melons do a kamikaze dive off the back, he plucks one from the top of the pile. It's nearly a perfect oval, deep green all the way around the middle, fading to yellow where he'd snipped it off the vine a couple of hours before. Balancing it on his knee, Jake slaps it, listening for that hollow *thunk* to tell him the fruit is firm, not overripe. He reaches in his back pocket and slides out his single-blade knife. Flipping it open, Jake slices the watermelon in one smooth circular motion. Then he pulls the two halves apart so they split with a crisp crack.

The fruit at the center is bright red and fades to pink next to the white rind. No matter how ripe, watermelons always smell like cucumber right after the first cut. Then as soon as the juice dribbles onto his jeans or on his hand, the sugary sweet smell makes his mouth water. Sometimes farming could be pretty dang monotonous, but cutting into a fruit or vegetable, full-grown from one puny seed, never failed to amaze Jake.

He sets the two watermelon halves on top of the pile so they stare out at the highway. Then he pulls the melon sign from the passenger side of the cab and leans it up against the bed of the pickup truck. In a way, the sign is overkill. If folks driving by can't figure out what he is selling in the back of his truck, they're either from another planet or they probably aren't looking to buy any watermelons. But it's tradition.

When Jake was little, his mom took scrap plywood from around the farm and painted each piece white. Every crop had its own sign. She wrote MELONS or TOMATOES or CORN in black letters, big, across the top. Then Jake painted the fruit or vegetable at the bottom of the sign. Every spring, they'd freshen up the signs together. Now his little sisters, Jessica and June-Bug, are starting to add their artistic touches to the signs. Jake had noticed that the tomatoes looked suspiciously like hearts.

He can still see the faded dollar sign under the white paint and an unidentifiable number. His dad asked them to stop locking in the prices with paint many years before. That was back when his older brother, mom, and dad would come to the pull-out and sell the produce together. Now, his brother's off at college. His mom's at home with his two little sisters and his dad manages their satellite farm sixty miles away.

Every Saturday, Jake asks his little sisters to come with him. They want to come, and Jake bet his mom he could keep them busy for six hours. After all, he and his brother did the whole six-hour stint when they were way younger than his eight- and six-year-old sisters. But his mom is freaked out about the murder last month and Tommy's disappearance two months ago. In fact, she's lobbying hard to sell produce someplace else. Jake's pretty sure his dad will wait the worry out.

He looks around the pull-out. Funny how small it seems now. He used to race his brother end to end and it seemed like he'd never get to the other side. Now he circles the whole thing in a minute. Ever since he found Tommy Smythe's dirt bike stashed under the cedars two months ago, Jake walks around the pull-out every Saturday. If the trash can is dumped over, he rights it and picks up trash, if there is any. Truth be told, he's keeping an eye out for any signs of Tommy. He still feels bad that he didn't go out and look for Tommy that very day he found the bike.

When he called the Smythes to tell them he'd found it, they drove out immediately. They said Tommy had been missing since school got out the day before. They were kind of freaked out. Mrs. Smythe thought they should leave the bike in case he came back. Mr. Smythe didn't want the bike stolen. Jake didn't think there was anything to worry about. It'd been less than a day. He told them Tommy was probably camped out some-where on the Stillwell Ranch. Jake felt bad that he didn't get more worried right away. It just seemed that a kid like Tommy might wander off, get distracted, and maybe lose his way for twenty-four hours. Now that he's been missing for two months, Jake wishes he'd driven his truck out in the field to look for him right then. He could have. They could have climbed in his truck and driven the ranch together. Instead, he helped the Smythes load Tommy's bike in their car and watched while Mr. Smythe called Sheriff Caldwell on his cell. Mrs. Smythe sat in the car crying.

The more Jake thinks about how he didn't jump in the truck and look for Tommy, the worse he feels. He hates how he waits around for things to happen. If that had been his brother or little sisters, Jake hopes he would have done it differently. At least he showed up for every search that Sheriff Caldwell organized.

Jake didn't really know Tommy. He knew who he was. He seemed like a mini-genius but kind of odd, especially the way he would sit and stare at things, even people. He'd seen him drive by on that red dirt bike. Fast. Then he'd stop. Like almost in the middle of the road and stare. Jake couldn't tell if Tommy was staring at him or particles in the air. Something. He was a strange kid. Still, he shouldn't have hesitated. Ever since that Saturday, Jake keeps watching out for Tommy. Sometimes Jake really hopes Tommy will show up. Mostly he hopes Tommy will show up so he can stop feeling guilty about not looking right away.

Jake glances at his watch. Ten thirty. He probably has an hour before his first customers show up. Every fruit and vegetable has a best selling time. Watermelons sell better after noon. Cucumbers and tomatoes sell better in the morning. He's tried to convince his dad of this phenomenon but he won't have it. "Jake, we need to be there the same time every Saturday. Ten to four. Consistency is the key." Jake doesn't argue but he makes sure to tell his dad whenever his theory proves correct.

Today, it looks like he could get a little nap before his first customer. Jake walks back to the cab and climbs into the passenger side. He leans back and stretches his legs out so they rest on the door hinge. To someone driving by, this probably looks like the quintessential Texas scene. A pickup full of watermelons and some farmer in blue jeans with his boots hitched over the door. A photographer might slam on the brakes and take a picture thinking he's capturing the essence of Texas. He'd have no idea that this particular farmer is a high school graduate who isn't sure he wants to be a farmer.

Problem is, farming is all Jake knows. That's what the Travers family is famous for: fruits and vegetables in the spring, summer, and fall; pies and canned goods in the winter. His brother went to A&M to study agriculture so he can join the family business. But Jake isn't sure. He feels stuck. He graduated from high school but he doesn't know what he wants to do. It seems like everyone else has a plan. His counselor made him apply to Shreiner, the liberal arts college about forty-five minutes away. He got in. He claimed his spot for the fall but he still isn't sure he wants to go. Shouldn't he know what he wants to study before he goes? Or maybe he should go and figure it out.

One of the cool things about farming is the seed knows exactly what it's going to be. Yeah, Jake has to water and weed it, and worry about cold snaps and droughts, but if everything goes according to plan, that tomato seed produces a bunch of tomatoes. There's no uncertainty or wondering. The seed doesn't have to figure out what it wants.

Honk. Honk. "Yo, Jake!"

Jake opens his eyes and looks at the car next to him. Four

yahoos from Fred High, crammed into a maroon Trans Am, pull up next to him.

The driver leans out his window. "Hey, Jake, how much will you charge us for four watermelons?"

Jake unhooks his legs from the door and stands up but they're dead asleep. He leans back on the seat until the blood rushes into his legs. "Twenty bucks."

"Five bucks a melon? How much if I buy one?"

"Five bucks."

"Aww, man. Come on."

As soon as his legs stops tingling, Jake walks over to the Trans Am. He recognizes the driver. His dad owns Clark's Salvage Yard. What's his name? Oh yeah, Alvin. He glances in at the others. He only recognizes the Mexican kid in the back. Nando. His dad Enrique helps on the farm a lot. Nando nods at Jake but doesn't say anything. Jake knows the nod. High school code for knowing someone but not really acknowledging that you know him.

"You can't be asking for discounts at the beginning of the day, Alvin. Come back at four. I might sell you the whole bed for twenty bucks."

"Fuck, yeah!" Alvin high-fives the kid in the passenger seat.

"I *might*. Probably won't. But I'll definitely give you a discount. What do you want with four watermelons anyway? A circle jerk?"

"Whoa! Does that even work?" asks Alvin.

"Cost you twenty bucks to find out."

"Seriously, man. I'm asking. Have you ever done it?" Alvin's eyes shift from Jake to the watermelons. It looks like he's trying to assess whether or not Jake is pulling his leg or if it is, in fact, possible to plunge his dick into the guts of a watermelon.

Jake smiles. "I highly recommend it. Seedless is better. You can scratch the shit out of yourself on those seeds."

"Are those seedless?" Alvin asks.

"Mostly."

Alvin looks at the other guys. They're all listening. "Well, like how do you do it?"

Jake can't help but laugh. "Wait. You guys don't know how to jerk off?"

Everyone in the car but Alvin laughs. Jake sees his face flush red. "Fuck you. That's not what I'm asking. I'm asking about, you know, how you do it with the watermelon."

"Oh, you want my recipe for watermelon delight? That might cost you more than twenty bucks."

"You're fucking with me. You've never jerked off in watermelon or a peach or a potato."

"A peach, yes. Once the pit is removed. Very satisfying. A potato, no, unless it is cooked, mashed, and cooled. Also quite delightful." Jake is having too much fun to stop. He can see Nando in the back trying not to laugh. Unfortunately, Alvin is not laughing. Jake had heard stories about his old man's temper. And his drinking. He backs off. "Seriously, Alvin, why do you need four watermelons?"

"We're going down to the arroyo behind Nando's house to use 'em for target practice."

"Wouldn't cans be cheaper?"

"Yeah, but they jump around too much. You're always chasing 'em down. Watermelons are cool cuz you can start big and then keep shooting smaller and smaller pieces."

"So start with one for five dollars. If you still want more at the end of the day, come back and I'll sell you two for five."

"Deal." Alvin pops out of the Trans Am and walks around to the back of Jake's pickup.

"Here. Let me get you one that might be a little green." Jake digs out a melon from the front corner of the bed.

Alvin hands Jake five dollars and hefts the melon onto his shoulder. "Hey, man, can I ask you something?"

Jake nods.

"Are you going to college?"

"I haven't decided. Why?"

"I'm gonna be a junior next year and that's when they start talking to us about college. My old man says school's a waste of time. But I'm not so sure. You know I built that car?"

"No shit?"

"Yeah, I rebuilt that kid Tommy's bike."

"Wow, I didn't know that." Jake is impressed.

"Yeah. So I'm wondering if I need to go to college. Or even finish high school. Like, what can I learn there if I already know how to make a living?" Alvin turns to walk back to his car. "But then, I was talking to that kid Tommy and he knew some really wild shit, so it made me think that, you know, maybe I should think about it. Like maybe I could be more than a car mechanic. I don't know. It's probably a stupid question. I thought since you graduated that maybe you might be able to tell me if it was worth it."

Jake leans on the bed of the pickup. What should he tell Alvin? He doesn't want to bullshit him but he also doesn't have a very good answer. "Hey, man, I don't know. I mean, I wish I could tell you that it all made perfect sense and that high school made a difference. But I can't. I don't know what I'm gonna do. I think I'll figure it out. Some days, it's about getting up and doing the next thing, right?"

"Yeah, I guess I wish it was more certain." Alvin opens the car door.

"Me too. But hey, there's always watermelon delight."

"Fuck, yeah. I'll get back to you on that one."

Alvin starts the Trans Am with an unnecessary roar. Jake doesn't like those muscle cars but he's impressed that Alvin built this one. He'd never said two words to this kid in high school. True, Alvin is two grades behind him, but still, who knew that he could build cars? Not only that, even with a pretty awesome skill, he feels the same purposelessness that Jake feels. Maybe it's okay, not knowing what the next step is. Maybe it's normal.

Jake watches the Trans Am pull away. Nando is looking at him. Jake sees him wave a little. Maybe he feels more comfortable acknowledging that he knows Jake. Or maybe Jake seems cooler after joking around with them about watermelons. He shakes his head. That kind of thinking drives Jake nuts. That was high school. He is done with overthinking shit like that. Maybe he's overthinking his future. Maybe he should just make a choice and see what happens.

He walks over to the cab of the pickup. Just as he is about to sit down, he hears another car turn in. It's a light green minivan. The driver, a woman, pulls in at the opposite end of the pull-out and hops out. Right behind her, a little boy scrambles out of the van. He looks to be June-Bug's age, maybe five or six.

"I gotta go, Mom. Now."

"Okay, honey, let's go behind the bush."

"I wanna go by myself."

"Travis . . ."

"Mom . . ."

Jake points to a break in the cedars near the two logs that lay askew along the edge of the pull-out. "Private restroom right behind those cedars."

Travis looks at Jake. "See, Mom?" He runs off.

The mother sighs.

Jake knows that exhale of breath from his own mother. "Don't worry. There's no cliff back there."

She smiles at Jake. "What about poison ivy?"

"Not sure about that."

The mother looks after her little boy. She takes one step and stops. "Oh well, if he gets it, he gets it."

"He'll never get it again."

The mother laughs. "That's for sure." She reaches into her purse and pulls out a wallet. "How much for a melon?"

"Five dollars."

"Could you pick it out for me? I always seem to get them overripe or too green."

"Sure. No problem."

Jake slaps and thumps a few of the melons. He tends to pick the ones that have the most hollow *thunk* sound. Problem is they could be too green. He pulls one from the pile. "This one might be all right."

"Great. Would you put it in the back of the van?" She turns to the bushes. "Travis, are you okay?"

"I'm peeing on ants, Mom. It's so cool."

Jake walks around to the back of the van and opens the door. Just as he sets the melon down, a head pops over the back seat. A girl.

Jake jumps a little. "Oh sorry, I didn't know there was anyone else in here."

The girl stares at him. Jake doesn't think she is in high school yet. She looks a little too young, too pudgy, but she has eye makeup glopped on and is sporting a "Who do you think you are?" look on her face. Jake had barged into that expression dozens of times in high school. Girls have a unique way of sizing you up and dismissing you in a split second.

Instead of looking away like he did in high school, he braces the watermelon in the back of the van and looks at her. "Let me guess. You're going into high school next year."

She blushes. "How'd you know?"

"A talent." Jake doesn't say the talent comes from years of crushing on girls from afar, trying to find out everything about them so he could ask them out, only to be shot down because they weren't interested in him. Maybe if he had walked up and asked them out right away, he would have had better success. Or it might not have hurt so much when they said no.

The girl hangs her head over the back of the seat watching him, kind of like a little kid would. Except she isn't. Or she's trying not to be.

"Did you go to Fred Johnson High? I mean, Fred High?"

"Just graduated."

"Oh wow. Did you like it?"

Jake knows that his street cred had gone up by telling her he'd graduated. Maybe that's why it seems like everyone, well, two people, are asking his advice today. Maybe he should try to tell her something important. Or wise. Something that might make high school easier. Or more fun.

"It was okay." Jake rolls his eyes inwardly. Oh that's brilliant. "I mean, there are good and bad days like any school." Man, he is sounding stupider and stupider. He smiles a little at the girl. She doesn't smile back. She looks like she is trying to figure out if he is cool or if he is a loser selling melons on the side of the road. He really wants to say something that will make high school better for her. "I mean, the worst part of high school is always trying to act way cooler or more together than you feel." Jake slaps the melon. "Just be the melon if you're the melon. Don't try to be a peach or a tomato. If you're a melon, be the best darn melon you can be. That's this loser's advice about high school." He smiles at her. Her face is blank. Jake closes the back door of the van. Well, at the very least, she'll always remember him when she's eating a melon.

The mother is standing near the cedar break under a scrawny branch of a mesquite tree. The sunlight through the leaves speckles her arms. "Travis, honey. Are you about done?"

"Yeah, I guess so. I'm watching the ants swim in the river I made."

"Travis, let's go."

Jake slides his pocketknife out, flips it open, and cuts a big circular slice off the cut melon. "Hey, Travis, got a slice of melon for you."

"Really?" Travis scurries through the cedars. "I love watermelon."

Jake smiles. That kid makes him think of his little sisters. It's so simple for them. They run around doing little-kid stuff. They think of something, they do it. They don't question if they should or shouldn't.

"Oh, you don't have to do that." The mother reaches into her purse. "Let me pay you."

"I don't charge for slices." Jake breaks the slice in half and gives one piece to Travis. "Here you go." Jake hands her the other slice. "I have to cut one open anyway."

"That's awfully nice of you. All right, Travis, let's go. No seed spitting in the car."

"Aww, Mom."

"Especially not at your sister."

"Aww, Mom."

"Travis . . ."

"Okay . . ."

Jake watches the boy climb in the van and the mother shut the door behind him. He can remember being that small, with his feet sticking straight out from the seat, not touching the floor or the seat in front of him. He can remember not being able to see a darn thing. Not out the window in front or right next to him. He'd watch the sky go by. Sometimes he'd count telephone poles. But that game always made him fall asleep.

As the van turns around and accelerates out of the pull-out, Jake raises his hand to wave goodbye. When he realizes the mom isn't looking at him and Travis can't see out the window, Jake starts to put his arm down, feeling stupid. Except the girl *is* staring at him. The watermelon is in her hand. Jake waves and smiles. Maybe she's thinking about being the melon.

Jake walks over to the truck and leans onto the hood under the shade. This next step isn't such a big deal. It's just a step. It gets so built up. Life after high school. College. Job. Career. Lasting relationship. Maybe that girl in the van is thinking the same thing about life after middle school, that high school is this really big deal. It's not. It's school. It's hanging out. It's finding your spot with people you like. It's getting through awkward times.

Maybe Jake is the one who makes everything more momentous than it needs to be. Like the way he waited too long to ask Kimmie Jo to the prom. He kept second-guessing the way she looked at him. By the time he figured out she might want to go, he heard she was already going with some other kid in her class. It wasn't a big deal. He didn't have a crush on her. But she was cute. And talkative. Jake liked girls who could hold up their end of the conversation. But he blew it by hesitating. Like not going after Tommy right away.

Jake walks to the other side of the pull-out. What if he is still driving out here in fifty years with watermelons in the back of his truck? Jake imagines his waist thickened like his father's. He can almost see his tan turning into those liver-colored splotches that stretch up and down his dad's arms. He can feel his father's hunched-over gait in his own muscles from years of walking in the fields, bending over, looking at the plants. Jesus, what a creepy picture. What if he never feels that little-kid excitement about wanting something ever again? What if he does and he blows it by hesitating?

At the opposite end of the pull-out is a decent-sized boulder, tucked under a mesquite tree. Jake sits down and looks at his truck. Everything is right in front of Jake but he can't feel the want of going toward something. How do you get that feeling of wanting something? And going after it. Maybe if he goes to college, the want will happen.

"Shit." His voice interrupts the silence of the pull-out. Jake wishes he could stop his stupid wonderings about his life. He closes his eyes and feels the burn of tears inside his eyelids. The sun is going to move across the sky like it always does. The next crop will grow, then the harvest, then the planting. Maybe it doesn't matter if he never feels the want of going after something.

He watches the truck and the watermelons. In his mind's eye, he can see himself sitting in the cab with his legs hooked over the door hinge. He can also see himself sitting on the rock watching his truck. In that one moment, he is both Jakes. One of them wanting to wait and see. The other wanting to go for it. He feels torn between the two.

Just then, a light blue pickup sails into the pull-out, not slowing for the ruts and bouncing right out of them. It skids to a stop next to Jake's truck. It looks like a miniature version of the same truck. The two together make Jake think of that game in his sisters' *Highlights* magazine, the one where they circle the differences in two side-by-side pictures. Other than size, these two trucks look identical. Yep, even the taillights—red, white, red—are stacked up the same way.

The driver's door opens and a girl steps out. Her hair is clipped up on top of her head and sunglasses shade her eyes. She is wearing a Fred High T-shirt, jean shorts, and boots.

Jake squints. He knows her. Genie McAllister. She graduated a year ahead of him. He remembered the one time he spoke to her. It was her senior year. She was walking down the hall. He was coming out of a classroom, late. He bashed into her and knocked all the books she was carrying onto the floor. He was so apologetic. He kept dropping everything he picked up. She smiled at him and said, "It's all right."

That was when Jake noticed her cowboy boots and the curve of her legs under her jeans. She was all curves. From the waves in her auburn hair to the sweater that hugged her waist. She was tall. They were standing eye to eye. He said "I'm sorry" one more time and she put her hand on his shoulder and said, "It's okay. Really. No harm, no foul." Then she walked away.

Jake watched her walk down the hall. From that moment until she graduated, Jake kept track of Genie McAllister. He knew when she had a class on the science hallway. Or math. Or English. He knew which period lunch she had. He kept her in his peripheral vision. How had he never noticed her before? He knew the McAllister family. He knew they had a daughter named Genie. But it's like he'd never seen her before.

Once he did, he imagined dating her. She seemed so different from all the other girls at Fred. Friendly, bold, direct. Not one ounce of the confusing coyness that drove Jake nuts. She seemed like she knew exactly who she was. He imagined asking her out. He imagined that she would say yes. He imagined it every night. Talk about watermelon delight. One time, he fantasized about running into her again, having a conversation with her, being bold enough to ask her out. He even went so far as to figure out what classroom he needed to be leaving in order to accidentally run into her. But he worried it wouldn't be the same. He would know it was coming. He'd be expecting her to act the same way. If she didn't, well, he didn't want to ruin it. So he kept imagining it all the way to the end of the year, when she graduated and went to UT.

Now she is standing in the pull-out. She is looking around, peering into the cab of his truck. She walks around the truck. Eventually she stops by the watermelons. She slaps a few. Picks up a few more.

"Hello? Anybody around? I want to buy a watermelon." She reaches into her front pocket and pulls out some bills. She ducks inside the cab and puts the money on the dashboard. Then she lifts one of the greenest watermelons into her arms.

Too green. Even at this distance, Jake is pretty sure it isn't the sweetest one. Jake wants to help her get the best one. He stands up and starts walking toward her. He doesn't want to startle her so he scuffs his boot and kicks a rock so it trips across the caliche. She turns and smiles.

That smile.

Jake can hear her explaining how the money is in the truck. He smiles at her. "No harm, no foul."

I think we create a God because life is mysterious. We don't understand the space in between the particles so we fill it with God. If some supreme being is responsible for all the spaces in between, then we don't have to be afraid of the mysteries. Like God is some shield against fear.

Except everyone is still afraid. Which is weird, because if there was some supreme being who created the Higgs field, which caused matter to create mass and gravity and life as we know it, then that supreme being would also create an intelligence big enough to conceive of it, big enough to hold all kinds of possibilities, big enough to see all the connections, big enough to see the spaces in between and not be afraid.

Hawking said we don't have to dismiss the existence of God when we talk about the creation of the universe. God can exist. But it may not have anything to do with the creation of the universe. Wouldn't it be better if the creation of the universe is determined by the laws of science, so that religion and faith can exist separately?

TIM

NO, I DON'T MIND TAKING A BREAK, SHERIFF. IT'S hot as hell out here. I swear the main part of the preseason workout is surviving the heat.

I can't really tell you much about Tommy. I mean, I only saw him when I was going into McCloud's classroom after school. That's where I met Izzy for tutoring. I was flunking out of regular physics. If I fail anything, I can't play sports. And if I can't play sports, I'm not going anywhere.

I started going back in January. Like I said, I didn't meet Tommy. He was either gone or leaving as I was getting there. He was kinda rude, the way he'd blow past me. About the third time it happened, I said something like "Dude, yoo-the-fuck-hoo. Say 'Excuse me,' why don't you?" I swear he looked at me like I was speaking Greek and kept going.

That's when Izzy told me his name. Said he always bolted class the minute the bell rang. She seemed kind of protective of him. At first I thought there was something there. You know, like maybe Izzy liked him, but then I figured out it was a big sister kind of thing.

He seemed okay. Definitely nerdy but not a jerk like that guy James. That dude is offensive. Tommy was weird, like he was tuned in to another channel.

That's as much as I know. I went there maybe twice a week to do my homework before practice. Izzy really helped me. I got to play basketball and baseball. Yeah, I'm a jock: football in the fall, basketball in the winter, and baseball in the spring.

I never would have noticed Izzy if she wasn't tutoring me. Not that she's not pretty. She is, but she's totally different from the other girls I know at Fred. That's why I liked her. She isn't always talking about her hair and makeup or her skin-cleaning routines.

Yeah I went by there that Friday. Not for tutoring. To see Izzy. To ask her to the prom. Tommy definitely wasn't there. I waited until I was pretty sure she was alone. It was a week before the prom. A little late to ask someone, I know, but I was trying to make sure she wasn't seeing anyone. I listened to her and Rachel talk while I was doing my homework. I watched what she did between classes. You know, I figured it out.

Okay, so I probably should admit it. I read that kid Tommy's journal. Back in April, a month or so before he disappeared. That's when I thought about asking Izzy to the prom but I wasn't sure if she was seeing someone. When I saw Tommy's journal lying on the floor like it had fallen out of his backpack, I picked it up. I looked at one page and saw that he'd written "her" and "she" a bunch of times. So I took it home and read it. I thought maybe he was writing about Izzy. I mean, he saw her every day, so I thought maybe he would write about her. If I saw her every day, I'd write about her. If I kept a journal, that is. I mean. Isn't that what you're supposed to write about in journals: girls?

He wrote about weird shit. Stuff I couldn't understand. Like about simultaneous realities and multiple universes and an original particle that started this whole world. I can tell you one thing for certain. That guy does not believe in the God my mom believes in. If her church got ahold of that journal, they would have burned it.

No way I kept it. Not in my house. I snuck it back into McCloud's classroom and put it on his desk. I assume he gave it back to Tommy. I never saw it again.

Not a word about Izzy. Nothing. Turns out the "her" was Rachel. It was pretty scientific but you could tell he liked her. Like the way he described her hair. It wasn't brown; it was this color of sand by a certain creek out on the Stillwell Ranch after it rained. At a certain time of year. No wonder the dude didn't pay attention to where he was going. He had formulas of brown in his head.

After I read the journal, though, I thought about how all I talk about is basketball and football and stats. Like we all have stuff we're really focused on. Tommy's thing is particle physics and alternate dimensions and the color brown. My mom is all about God and good and evil and doing everything the Bible says. The thing is, we're not that different except in how we think about life. Do you see what I mean? It's like we get fixated on how we look at the world. But we're all doing the same thing: looking at the world. You know, trying to understand it through the things we like.

I'm not saying I believe what Tommy wrote. I probably didn't understand it. But all he was trying to do was figure out stuff through how he looked at the world. The way my mom looks at it through her church. Some people think God created this world. Some people think there was a big bang. What if it was both? What if we never know because we can't go back in time to find out? What if it doesn't matter?

People like Tommy and Izzy and that whole junior nerd squad, they want to explore every possibility. They want to find out the truth through science and observation and experiments. But when I go to church, I hear words like "faith" and "hope" and "belief." It makes me wonder if science is kind of limited. Maybe there are supposed to be mysteries we can't explain. Or shouldn't explain.

I didn't read every word in the journal, but I didn't see anything about Tommy planning to run away or meet someone. Besides, he seemed more like an in-the-moment kind of guy, not a planner. I'm in the moment when I'm playing ball, but I'm also playing offense and planning shit out. Like with Izzy, I was checking out if she was going out with anyone and planning out when to ask her to the prom, so that once I asked her I was ready for all the possibilities in the moment.

Like I noticed her talking in the library with this computer nerd Alex. So I asked around about him and found out that they grew up across the street from each other. So I figured they were friends. Someone told me he crushed on her in middle school but it was over. Besides, he's kind of lame looking. A real beaky nose and his head looks like it was squeezed in a doorway.

I thought maybe she liked that guy James but no way. Like I said, he's an ass. Besides, I don't think he went in for girls.

Because the dude hit on me. It was late April. Fred High had made it into the division baseball finals. I was doing my physics homework and he sat down next to me. Izzy was helping someone else at another table. Anyway, he started talking to me and telling me that unless he walked into the gym and observed me hitting a ball, there was an equal possibility that I wasn't hitting a ball. Not only that, in some sort of quantum guru world, there could be a zillion balls being hit as long as no one was there to observe it. I said, "So what?" Like why bother thinking about all the possibilities that you don't see? It's purposely confusing.

He said, "Because the possibilities are what will blow your mind." And then he put his hand on my leg under the lab table. Not like an accident. He was rubbing my thigh. No lie. When I jumped up and told him to knock it the fuck off, he acted like it didn't happen. Like it was one of the many possibilities, but if no one saw it, then it was only a possibility. I stayed away from him after that.

I listen to the nerd squad and I don't know why they're the smart ones. According to them, if you didn't observe what happened to Tommy, then all possibilities exist: He's dead. He's kidnapped (and possibly dead or alive). He's lost. He's found his bio parents and is living with them. He's found another dimension. I said, "Well, isn't that a mystery?" No, they don't believe in mystery. To them, it's all probability. They think they're so smart. I think they're confused.

I know you have to look at it logically and check out every possibility, Sheriff. I guess I feel stupid around them. It doesn't seem like Tommy could be alive after this long. I mean, look how many people die crossing over from Mexico. Ranchers find them in their fields all the time. I know you haven't found his body. And I know he was missing almost twenty-four hours before you started the searches, but he couldn't disappear in thin air, right? But he could have walked a long way. He could have gotten really thirsty. He could have passed out. Someone could have found him. He could be alive but he might not re-member who he was. I mean, he was a pretty strange guy. Maybe dehydration would have made him stranger.

This whole thing with Tommy disappearing makes you question everything. Like what you believe. My mom says we should pray. If we pray enough to God, then Tommy will turn up. That doesn't seem right either. I mean, what does God have to do with it? Why does one supreme being care?

I guess I believe that life is really random and mysterious. I guess I believe that science and God can't explain everything because life is random.

Like feelings. Like how I like Izzy? That was random. What about how we kissed at the prom? That was random. I mean, it's pretty random that a jock would like a geek. But it happened.

What about that pickax girl? Wasn't that random?

Some stuff is random. Feelings. Violence. Scoring more

baskets than you ever have before. Why can't that be random and mysterious? Why does it have to be probable or possible? Why does there have to be some equation for it? Why does everything have to be linked to something else?

Like the day I took Tommy's journal. I'd seen it on the floor before. But I took it that day. Why? Does it matter why?

Like the way my mom brings meals over to Tommy's house. Nobody asked her. Nobody organized it. She just does it. Isn't that random? Maybe she does it because it makes her feel good. Or maybe she does it because she's afraid that someone will snatch me and if she does good things, then she'll keep the bad things away. What if she's trying to pay off God with her goodness? What if it is goodness for goodness' sake, like she's trying to put good back in the world? We don't know. It's random. It's mysterious. Why can't we just let it be?

Tommy believed in the mysterious. From what I read. I mean, a lot of it was science and probabilities, but he said there have to be mysteries because that's what science wants to explore. Like he goes on and on about black holes and holes to other dimensions, how nothing's proved, how anything is possible. Well, isn't that mystery?

Izzy, James, even McCloud, they want to explain it all. Sometimes the way they talked made me feel like fruit flies were buzzing around my head. I wanted to say something but I didn't. It would probably sound stupid. All that science talk makes me feel stupid. Probably you shouldn't like a girl who makes you feel stupid, right? But that's what they can't explain. Liking someone is a mystery.

Yeah, I still like her. I saw her a couple of times over the summer. We didn't kiss like we did at the prom but I still like her. I don't know if I'll need tutoring again this year but if I do, I hope she'll do it. I have to keep playing so I can get recruited.

Does there have to be a reason for my liking her?

Can't it be random?

When we die, our bodies are as active as when our cells are dividing right after conception. The energy of being alive doesn't go away. It becomes a different form of matter. Even in cremation. The body gets transformed into another kind of matter. The energy of a body, dead or alive, doesn't dissipate.

RITUAL

THE MINUTE SHE AND HER MOTHER STOP AT THE pull-out, Tara knows it's a mistake.

"I don't know why you want to look at this place," her mother says. She parks the car so it's facing toward the highway as if she wants to make a quick getaway.

Tara doesn't say anything as she opens the door and gets out. She isn't sure why she wants to stop or what she's going to see. Her dad's murder happened two months ago. It wasn't like blood would still be splattered everywhere or there'd be a taped outline of his body on the dirt like the *Law & Order* shows she'd watched.

It's empty. The caliche is white hot under the August midday sun. It hurts her eyes it's so bright. Even the cedar trees ringing the pull-out are dusted with caliche like a freak snowstorm had blown through this one spot.

Who knows? Maybe it had snowed. Maybe the whole universe

had been altered and it snowed in August in Texas. Why else would she be standing in a pull-out looking for her dad's blood? Why else would her dad be stuffed in a sack in the backseat? Why else was her mother bringing home endless burgers from the Whip In and not even eating them?

Yes, that has to be what's happened. The whole world has been knocked slightly out of its orbit and everything's been off course since Tommy disappeared. That's how she felt the first time she came out of her chemistry class and Tommy wasn't walking down the hall toward her. That's where she always saw him, hurrying down the hallway. Sometimes he was writing something in his notebook. Sometimes he was reading a book. Always his backpack was unzipped. Always it seemed like he'd been interrupted. Tara looked for him every day until the end of school. Out of habit. Out of hope. Then her dad was murdered. Yes, the whole world went wobbly.

Tara looks over at the car. Her mom hasn't moved. Her hands are still on the steering wheel like she's still driving down the road, eyes forward. That's how she looked the whole trip to the crematorium. Tara had forced her mom to go. The crematorium had called every week since the middle of June. Her mom had heard the messages even though she refused to answer the phone.

"Mom, they're going to keep calling. We have to go." Truth was, all Tara wanted to do was put her world back together before school started. Picking up the ashes seemed like a good first step.

"You go by yourself."

"I don't have my license yet."

"Who cares? You know how to drive. It'll be one more illegal thing this family has done."

There it was again. Every conversation ended here: her dad's betrayal. At first when the sheriff called, all she and her mom knew was that there had been an accident. Then he was dead. Then murdered. Bit by bit, the news of her dad's secret life came out. Neither of them had known about the drug business her dad had going. At least Tara didn't. She couldn't tell if her mom knew or not because she was so mad. When the sheriff told them that the girl who killed him was a seventeen-year-old prostitute he'd had an affair with, her mom went over the edge. When the whole story came out in the paper, her mom gave up stopping at the Whip In. She went straight up to her room with a bottle of wine and drank until she passed out. Tara was pretty sure that her mom rarely showered. As for the washing machine, Tara knew for a fact that she was the only one using it.

Tara walks back to the car. This whole trip has been a disaster. What did Tara expect? That her mom would snap out of her funk and they would bond over the ashes? Or that they would laugh about their morbid experience at the crematorium?

It went south the minute the receptionist tried to sell them an urn.

Her mom asked, "How much?"

"We sell all kinds. They start at one hundred dollars and go up from there."

"On top of what I'm paying you for the ashes?"

"Yes, ma'am."

"Just put 'em in a cardboard box," her mom said. "Or do I have to pay for that, too?"

"No, ma'am, I can find a box in the back."

Tara looked at the urns on the wall. She didn't really want an urn for her dad either. All of them looked like some version of the sports trophies outside the gym at Fred High. But when the woman came out with an old beat-up cardboard box and plopped the plastic bag of ashes in it, Tara thought it looked like someone had cleaned out a wood stove and the whole package was on its way to the dump. The way the lady was smiling, it looked like she knew who was in that box. It looked like she put all her meanness and judgment into choosing it and then capped it off with, "Have a nice day."

Her mom didn't seem to mind or notice. Maybe she liked that her drug dealing, cheating husband was in the crappiest cardboard box at the crematorium. The way her mom tossed it onto the backseat and slammed the door didn't lift the moment above an everyday chore.

Tara looks around the pull-out one last time and walks back to the car.

As soon as she opens the car door, her mom says, "We could dump the ashes right here where he died. Be done with it." Tara sits down. In the two minutes she had walked around the pull-out, the sun had heated up the vinyl seat. It seared the back of her legs. She focused all her thoughts on not flinching.

Tara looks over. Her mom's hands are still on the steering wheel but her eyes are closed and her head is back on the head-rest. Tara doesn't move or say anything. She knows if she doesn't get out and dump the ashes, her mom isn't going to do it. Tara keeps her mouth shut. She's figured out it's best not to argue with her mom or try to reason with her. Pretty soon, she'll be lying on her bed passed out.

"Goddamned son of a bitch."

"Mom . . ."

"Shit." Her mother shoves the gear in drive and accelerates hard out of the pull-out. She doesn't look to see if a car is coming. Tara knows her mom wouldn't have cared if a car smashed into them. She's barely hanging on to life or her sanity. Tara wonders if there is much difference between her dead parent in the sack and the one driving the car. She keeps trying to give her mom a lot of slack but it's hard. When is she going to snap out of it?

Like her mom, Tara avoids going into town as much as possible. She's glad the murder happened after school got out and she didn't have to face anyone's stares or listen to their whispers in the hallways. It happens enough going to the grocery store. All Tara has to do is look around as she's leaving and two or three customers are leaning together, whispering. The only person who is halfway normal to them is Sam at the Whip In. The first thing he said was, "Sorry for your loss, Mrs. Simmons. I'm real sorry, Tara." It's probably why her mom stopped there for food so often.

Tara hears the blinker clicking and looks down the highway. Her mother must have been speeding to get home as fast as they did. At the end of their driveway is a beautiful purple sign with her mom's script. Lavender Valley.

"We should paint that sign over. Black. I don't want people

stopping to buy lavender and snoop around anymore." She turns onto the driveway and speeds down it as fast as she can.

Again Tara doesn't say anything. They had already skipped the lavender festival and not harvested any flowers to make soaps or oils. Her mom has tears rimming her eyes and her hands are gripping the steering wheel so tight it looks like she might break it. In a way, her mom looks like she might explode and get swallowed by her own negative energy. Tara takes a deep breath, trying to bring calm into the car.

"Goddamnit, Tara, why'd you make me leave the house and go get those damn ashes?" Her mom shoves the car into park under the pecan trees by the front of their house. She stops short of crashing into her dad's Super Glide black custom Harley with the gold trim. It's still parked in the same spot from when her dad got home that night in June. Tara is surprised her mom hasn't hit it yet. Without a word, her mom goes into the house. Tara knows she is opening the refrigerator and taking the never-ending bottle of white wine up to her bedroom.

She reaches in the backseat and picks up the box with her dad's ashes. Before they'd learned about his secret life, she and her mom had one normal conversation about what to do with the ashes. They both agreed to put a cross by the lavender fields and bury them there. But now it seems like his whole lavender farm was a lie and Tara isn't so sure her mother won't put the ashes in the trash. In fact, it worries her. That's why she hides them up on the top shelf of the pantry.

That's why she gets up in the middle of the night to check on them.

She creeps downstairs and snaps on the pantry light. The

box is still there. She clicks off the light and turns to go back upstairs. Then she worries that maybe the bag isn't inside. She reaches up and pulls down the box.

The bag is still inside, plump with ashes. She holds it in her hand. It feels like a sack of flour, only looser, more crumbly. She wants to open it but she hesitates. It feels wrong to touch her dad's ashes, but then her fingers touch the twisty that closes the bag and it feels more wrong to have something as stupid and mundane as a twisty closing the bag that holds her dad. She untwists it and reaches inside.

This is him. This is his bones and flesh and hair all burned up and put in a sack. She didn't think it would feel like wood ashes or sand. But it feels like both. Except for the big clumps. They feel like bits of pitted gravel from the highway.

Tara holds the bag to her nose. It doesn't smell like anything. Not dirt or smoky ash. The plastic bag has more smell than her dad. She looks around the pantry. Maybe she should mix some cinnamon in with the ashes so he would smell like something. But she doesn't.

Instead she stands there holding him. She doesn't want to let go. She isn't sure her mom will ever want to touch his ashes, never mind bury them or spread them. But Tara does. She wants to do something. Ever since Tommy disappeared, day-to-day life felt uncertain. After her dad died, it felt a million times more wobbly. If she can figure out something special to do with the ashes, maybe she won't feel so out of balance.

Tara starts to put the ashes back but the house creaks and she stops. Her mom is up. Tara can hear her up and down a lot during the night. She steps into the kitchen and listens. The toilet flushes. Then footsteps pad across the floor. Then silence. Her mom is back in bed. She isn't coming downstairs for more wine. Tara stands there waiting for her mom to fall back to sleep. While she waits, she imagines filling another plastic bag with three scoops of ash from the wood stove. There's plenty. They save it after the winter to mix in with the soil. Two scoops of white caliche dirt from the edge of the driveway. The ash and caliche would be easy. The big bits of bone would be harder to fake. They couldn't look like pebbles. Maybe she could smash a big rock into different-sized pieces. Maybe.

Tara has no idea how long she stands in the doorway of the pantry. As long as it takes to make the plan to fake her dad's ashes. She reaches into a canister of used plastic bags, pulls out two or three, and stuffs them in the pocket of her bathrobe. Silent as the night, she climbs the stairs to her bedroom.

In her bed, Tara curls around the sack of ashes. At first, the plastic feels cold. Then it warms. She imagines the flames that ate her dad's flesh and bone. She imagines her father's body on a metal plate and the flames beneath him, roaring, turning his body white, then gold, then orange, until it disappears and falls bit by bit onto the tray below, where it cools to white and gray and gets put into this sack.

The last time she touched him was when she kissed him goodnight in June. They'd had a late supper because he'd just come home from his business trip and school was out. He asked if she wanted to go for a swim at the sinkhole and she said no. So did her mom. He looked disappointed but he sat on the porch and smoked his second cigarette of the day. He smoked one in the morning and one in the evening. It was his ritual he told her. One cigarette to think about what you want to do. And one cigarette to forgive yourself for whatever you didn't get done. Tara wondered what he was forgiving himself for that evening.

When it got late enough to go to bed, he came into her room and kissed her goodnight on her forehead. Tara never heard the phone ring in the night. She never heard him go downstairs or start his truck. She wondered if she would have heard him leave if he had started the Harley. In a way, he disappeared like Tommy. One day she saw him; the next she didn't. She never saw his dead body. It was almost like she could still wake up tomorrow and he would be there. If she didn't see his dead body, was he really dead? She touches the sack. Is this really him? One thing for sure is if she keeps lying next to that sack, that's what her memory of him will become. That's why she has to do something with the ashes. Tomorrow. She isn't sure what it will be. Something. Something special.

The next night, she creeps down the hall cradling two filled plastic sacks. Her mom's door is open. Tara looks in. She's sprawled across the bed, clothes still on. It looks like she passed out again. Tara thinks about leaving her a note but what would she say? "I've gone for a walk with Dad." No. Best just to go.

In the kitchen, she sets her father's ashes on the table and steps into the pantry. She clicks on the light and looks at the sack of fake mixture in her hands. It has the same heft and gray-ish color as the real sack, although the fake stuff is a little bit darker. The jagged pieces of rock look pretty similar to the bone fragments. If her mom ever pulls down the box and looks at the sack, she might not know, but if she opens it up, she'd smell the burned wood ash. If she remembers where Tara put the ashes. Her mom might leave this box right here forever and never dump them out. Or maybe when Tara goes off to college, she'll throw them in the trash. Maybe. Tara is pretty sure her mom isn't going to look in the box for quite a while. She can probably keep track of her mom's mental health by checking to see if the box is still in the pantry. It doesn't matter. Tara's decided what she is going to do.

She clicks off the pantry light and steps into the dark kitchen. First, she grabs her backpack hanging on the hook by the door. She unzips it and sets the ashes in the bottom. She hears paper crinkle and looks inside. At the bottom is a whole stack of flyers. Tommy's face looks up at her.

"This is my dad, Tommy. Maybe he knows where you are," whispers Tara. Then, as quietly as possible, she zips the backpack closed and turns the knob on the back door.

Outside, the crescent moon is already hanging low in the sky. It's a clear night. Tara heads for the back side of the barn and the bent fence post she knows is there. She doesn't want to open any gates too close to the house in case they creak and wake her mom. She pulls at the post and leans it toward her so a V-shaped opening appears where there isn't one before. Tara steps through it into the lavender fields.

She hadn't counted on the smell to hit her quite so hard. It stuns her to where she can't move. It's her dad. It's like he's all around her. Whenever Tara gave him a hug, he always smelled of lavender. His hair, his clothes, even the sweat on his neck. It doesn't seem possible that he is in a small plastic sack on her back. Tara pushes herself forward through the field. The lavender air caresses her skin. It isn't until she reaches the far side of the field that she notices she's been holding her breath and her face is wet with tears. As soon as she reaches the fence, she pulls herself over it and jumps. When she lands, she slips and falls back onto the dirt.

Tara looks up at the blanket of stars. She wonders, if one exploded, would all the other stars wobble in their orbits? Maybe only the closest ones. Maybe. Maybe it's totally normal for stars to fade away or burn out. Maybe a sudden absence is hardly noticeable.

It's different down here. When someone dies or disappears, everything changes.

Tara tried to keep everything the same after Tommy disappeared. She changed classes with her same group of girlfriends. She tutored in the freshman algebra classroom during lunch. She got rides home from school with Kimmie Jo. She went to the Whip In on Saturday afternoons after she volunteered at the animal shelter. She tried to keep everything normal. But it wasn't.

Tara was pretty sure she wouldn't see Tommy again. She couldn't explain why she felt that way. It was those last weeks of school, seeing his face on posters everywhere. Carrying around a stack of flyers and sticking them up whenever she stopped someplace that didn't have one. His face on the posters all over town became more real than her memory of him in the hallway.

That's how death is. It turns your world upside down. It makes what was real seem unreal. It pulls you out of normal. Makes you do things you've never done before. Like sit outside in the middle of the night with a bag full of your dad's ashes. When someone dies, your whole orbit changes.

Tara watches the stars. She knows they are exploding balls of gas. But they look cold. And immutable. If she watches long enough, could she see one of the stars explode? She wonders if it would look like a giant pickax smashing into its heart again and again. She wonders if the stars around it would shatter. Or if it would cause the Milky Way to spasm. Or would the stars continue to blink, like they're blinking right now? Staring at her. Witnessing what she is about to do.

Tara steps carefully through the tufts of grass and rocks and looks for the little cow trail that leads down to the sinkhole. This field is a lot like the one behind the Stillwell pull-out where they'd walked in a big long line looking for Tommy. Tara thought everyone would walk hand in hand across the field, but that wasn't how it was. They stood about six feet apart so they could cover more ground. Tara could hear some people talking. But most kept silent. It seemed like the time to be quiet. All the way along, Tara had to remind herself what she was doing. It was such a beautiful spring day. It didn't seem like the kind of day you'd come across a dead body. They didn't, of course, but if they had, Tara thought it should have been raining.

She spots the white ribbon of a trail curving around a stand of oak trees and heads for it. When she steps into the shadows of the trees, fear creeps up the back of her neck like the cool air lingering under the tree branches. She knows where she is going but she feels a little afraid. Her father had always been with her before. And now, even though he's with her, it doesn't exactly count. She stops and listens. When she doesn't hear anything like footsteps or rustling or the snap of twigs, she exhales.

Again, she thinks about Tommy. It's weird being out here to scatter her dad's ashes and Tommy keeps popping into her head. She wonders if he'd been scared right before he disappeared. Kids at school talked about him going into another dimension but Tara doesn't think it's possible. She wants to believe he's alive someplace. But now she isn't so sure. Bad things happen. Someone could be at the sinkhole right now. Tara might be attacked. Or killed.

Somehow, thinking of Tommy makes her less afraid. Like imagining the worst possible thing that could happen makes walking down to the sinkhole not so big and scary. Trying to push it away and pretend it isn't there makes it bigger. But if she names the fear and looks at it straight on, it stops scaring her. The worst possible thing that could happen is in her backpack. She tightens the straps and keeps walking.

When she first saw the sinkhole with her dad many years ago, she thought it looked like some thirsty monster had taken a bite of the earth to drink from the pool of water underneath. He told her there were lots of natural springs running underground. In some places, like this one, where the land slopes a little, the ground collapsed above a spring. At first, it looked like a gash. Now, with the trees growing up around it and grass creeping through all the rocks, it seems like it had always been there.

Tara kneels by the edge of the water. Hot from the walk or the fear or both, she scoops up a handful and rubs it on her face. Then her hair. Then her neck. She slides the backpack off, unzips it, and pulls out the ashes. When she first had the idea of coming out here, she thought she would empty her father's ashes into the pool. It seemed right to take him to the last place he wanted to go before he died. Maybe if they'd come here, he would have missed that call. Maybe.

Instead of emptying the bag into the water, she pours a small bit into her hand. She tries to remember what it felt like to hold her dad's big hands. She can see them in her mind. She can even see her smaller hand in his. But she can't remember what it felt like.

A gust of wind blows the ashes into the air. Some of them land in the water. The rest fall on the land, invisible to her.

Her dad's life had been invisible to her. She had no idea he had a secret life. He seemed happy and successful. The ups and downs of the lavender farm never seemed to bother him. When he went away, he always said he was building up business for their lavender products.

Even her mom seemed surprised. She said that he'd done drugs and ran with a pretty rough crowd. But that was before Tara was born. Her mom swore that he was done with it. That's why they moved to the country and started farming. Because he was done with that life. Because he was a father. She swore it. To Tara. To the police.

Tara pours another small bit of ashes in the palm of her hand and releases them into the water. They float on the surface for a bit and then gradually sink. In a way it's like watching him disappear when he left town. Tara remembers how he used to hug her so tight and tell her to be good and take care of her mom. He also whispered, "I love you, baby girl." Then he got on his Harley and rode away. Again and again.

How could her mom not know? He went away for such long stretches. Where did she think he was going? Sometimes, Tara felt infected by her mother's anger. She wanted to be sad that her dad was dead. But then she'd think about the girl who killed him. Tara saw her picture in the paper. She was only a year older than Tara. How could he make love with her? Did he make her fall in love with him by whispering, "I love you, baby girl," in her ear? Is that what made her want to kill him?

She reaches in the bag and takes out another handful. Maybe her dad has other families besides Tara and her mom. Maybe he has other baby girls. Maybe in a year, someone else will show up looking for him. Maybe Tara will have a half sister or brother.

Bit by bit she pours her father into the palm of her hand. One palmful, she blows into the wind. Another, she lets fall into the water. Another, she sprinkles on the ground. It seems fitting somehow that her dad is everywhere and nowhere; that she has made him disappear like he had disappeared on them.

When all that is left is one palmful of ashes, she closes her hand tight around them and puts her hand into the water. The water sneaks in between her fingers and the ashes slip out of her grasp. That's when she remembers how she would wiggle her small fingers in between her dad's big ones until she could feel his whole hand covering hers. Then she feels him slip away between her fingers like he'd always been slipping away but they never knew it.

He's gone.

Tara watches her empty hand float on the surface of the water. She still has to go to school and deal with all the questions and looks and whispers, but she isn't worried about it. This part is done. She said goodbye to her dad and the world didn't end. She hadn't realized until right then that she'd been afraid of falling into a black hole when she let her father's ashes go. That all the light and air would get sucked away when he was really gone. But it didn't happen. Maybe everyone needs to say goodbye to Tommy.

By the time Tara gets home, the crescent moon has set. She creeps upstairs and pauses outside her mother's bedroom. She can hear her snoring a little. Tara hopes she's taking a rest from all her anger. She wonders if her mother would ever be sad or remember good things about her father. She hopes so.

Tara goes into her room and lies down. When she finally falls asleep, she dreams of Tommy. She dreams she is looking out the window at the Milky Way. It looks like a stream of glittering ashes trailing across the sky and Tommy is floating in it.

I can't enter the world of the flower or the bug or the animal or even the mold spore. But I know each one exists. I can observe it. I know each one has its own reality. If they each had a consciousness, they would each have their own perception of that reality. But unless I can enter that consciousness or communicate with it, I can't enter it.

Yet I know they exist.

THE LAST DANCE

LIKE ALWAYS, FRANK STARTS BRAKING ON THE gravel road a good fifteen or twenty feet before it intersects with US 281, and, like always, the car skids a little on the pebbly surface. When it stops, he looks over at Stella. Like always, she has the visor down and is looking in the little mirror, fiddling with her hair.

"You know you don't need to do that."

"Do what?"

"Check yourself in the mirror. I can tell you if something's out of place."

"But then you couldn't keep your eyes on the road because I'd be asking you to look at me all the time."

"I'll take my chances." Frank glances in his rearview mirror. No cars are coming. He slides the gear into park and faces Stella. She is a beauty. A natural beauty. With high cheekbones and sparkling blue eyes that glint like the sunlight on water whenever she smiles. Frank loves to make her smile.

"You ready?" he asks.

Stella stops scooping her hair around her ears for a moment and stares at herself. Her hands slide down to her neckline and she pulls her light blue sweater closed, buttoning the top button. Then unbuttoning it.

Frank reaches over and puts his hand under her chin. He looks at her beautiful face. "Are you feeling all right, Stell?" Her eyes dart from his face to the windshield to her lap. He takes both her hands in his and asks her in a singsongy voice if she'd like to swing on a star and carry moonbeams home in a jar.

Like he hoped, it makes her smile. And giggle. She tips her face up toward Frank's and kisses him. He loves it when she does that: seals the moment with a kiss. It feels like an exclamation point after that smile. Both of them take Frank's breath away. But that smile is what he lives for. If he drew his last breath making that smile cross her face, he would die a happy, happy man. He leans into her lips, bending his head over hers, lingering in the kiss, and turning the exclamation point into a comma.

Honk. Honk. Honk.

Frank jumps away from Stella.

A car skids to a stop behind them and then pulls around, still honking. The driver yells, "Get a room," as he accelerates onto the highway.

Frank laughs. "Oh hell. Just when I was going to get a little."

"Frank!" Stella sounds embarrassed but she giggles.

"Shall we go to the dance, Stell?"

Stella turns around and faces front. She leans forward a bit, straining against her seatbelt, like she is willing the car forward. "Let's go, Frankie."

He slides the car into gear and eases it forward, looking both ways before turning north onto 281.

Frank rolls his window down. The sun is about to set. It's going to be a pretty evening. The glare of summer is over. Frank loves the early fall when the light is softer and the night comes on a little earlier. He reaches over and holds Stella's hand. He glances at her. She's leaning back a little bit. She looks a little bit more relaxed, as if the wheels moving farther down the road are unwinding the worry. That's what it looks like to Frank: worry. Kind of a high-strung, nervous worry. Sometimes he can't get her mind off whatever she's worrying about. Singing, talking, telling her a joke—that usually works. Asking her directly what's bothering her makes it worse. It's like drawing attention to a problem she can't fix. She starts grabbing at her collar or her skirt, and whatever thought is in her mind takes her over. Usually, he can hold her hand and that eases the worry some. Always, a drive brings her back to him.

"Frankie, do you think the Traverses are still at the pull-out? I want to stop and see what they have." She turns and looks out the back of the car. "We haven't passed it, have we?"

"No, it's up ahead. But it's way past their selling time."

"Would you stop anyway? I can say hello to Jean if she's there."

Frank knows the Traverses aren't going to be at the pull-out. Not only is it after six but it's Friday. He brakes and eases off the road, dropping into the ruts and divots. The car rocks from side to side as he pulls up next to a cluster of cedars.

Stella looks around. "Oh darn. They're not here. We need to come get our vegetables earlier, Frankie."

"You bet, sweetheart." Frank smiles at his beloved. He

would stop here at midnight and look for vegetables if it made her happy.

"It's so pretty right now." Stella opens her car door and gets out.

Before Frank can turn the car off, Stella walks toward the field and disappears between the cedars. He yanks the keys out of the ignition. Stella left her car door open. Frank thinks about closing it but goes after her instead.

"Stell?" He stoops to get under a low cedar branch, pushes his way through the undergrowth. "Stella? Are you okay?"

At first he can't see her. Then he spots her running across the field. He starts after her, yelling her name. She is about a hundred yards away from him. She isn't going very fast. Both of her arms are outstretched. She looked like a bird gliding over the field, but as Frank gets closer, he notices her gait is jerky and a couple of times she almost falls.

"Stella, stop!" he yells, and just like that, she stops and turns toward him. Frank doesn't know what to expect because he doesn't know what caused her to run across the field, but when she looks at him, she is smiling. As he walks up, her smile seems to grow brighter as her cheeks flush and her chest heaves from the running.

"Stella, what the—?"

"Frankie, I saw some deer in the field and I started walking toward them. Real quiet. They were watching me but they weren't running away. Then, all of a sudden, this big bird, a hawk or something, swooped down, and we all started running. I was running and running. The deer were so fast. Then I was running alone and I put my arms out like that big bird and I felt like I could fly."

"Oh, Stella." Frank pulls her into him so he can bend forward and kiss the top of her head.

"Did I look like I could fly?"

"I was worried you were going to fly away."

Stella giggles and smiles up at him. Then she looks into his eyes. Not quickly. She gazes at him as if his eyes steady her, as if she is walking a tightrope and his eyes are guiding her across the chasm between them. Frank knows this is his cue to kiss her. When he does, it's a free fall into her lips. He lets himself go and holds on to her. His arms tighten around her, pressing her whole body into him. They could be falling through space.

Frank shivers. Not from cold. From the thrill of standing next to her. How does she do that? He straightens up. "You got me again, Stella by starlight."

Stella nuzzles her nose into his chest. Pulling his shirt open a little.

"Come on now, Stella. We still got daylight."

"Aw, Frankie. We could go behind those bushes."

"Chiggers."

"Spoilsport."

"I do not want to paint nail polish all around my privates to kill little buggers ever again."

Stella laughs. "I thought my cotton candy pink looked pretty good on you."

"You are wicked." Frank slides one arm behind Stella and guides her back to the car. Stella leans into him. Even though

Frank is a good six inches taller, they fit together easily. They're made to walk next to each other. Or dance together.

Frank takes her hand and leads her through the ring of cedars at the edge of the pull-out, holding a few branches so they don't snap back in her face. When they step into the pull-out, a large black bird takes off from the crown of a live oak. Stella looks up.

"Oh there he is, Frank. The bird that chased the deer and me."

"That's a buzzard, Stell. Probably a dead animal nearby."

"Really? A buzzard?" Stella stares at the bird as it wheels in a wide circle above them. The black wings look like a cutout against the sunset-streaked sky. "They fly so pretty. You'd never know they were looking for dead things."

"We better keep moving so it doesn't get confused."

As Stella climbs in the car, Frank notices she isn't wearing her sweater. "Stella, did you leave your sweater in the field?"

"I don't think so."

"Are you sure? I'm pretty sure you were wearing it."

Stella smoothes the skirt of her dress. Again and again. Each time, she shakes her head back and forth. "I don't know."

Frank can see the worry line dig into the center of her forehead. He should go look for it. It might get colder. Blue northers can blow in real sudden, especially in September. He imagines the sweater lying on a tuft of grass like a small patch of blue fallen from the sky. But he doesn't want to leave her alone right then. He leans down and kisses her on the cheek. "I'll keep you warm, Stell."

As Frank accelerates out of the pull-out, clouds of caliche dust swirl behind the car. He can see the buzzard light on the trash can. It's watching Frank, waiting for him to leave, so it can eat the dead thing, wherever it is, in peace.

Frank looks over at Stella. Her hands are still smoothing her dress. He reaches over, takes one of them in his hand, and grips the steering wheel with his other hand a little tighter.

"What do you say we stop at the Whip In for a shake before we go to the dance?"

Stella doesn't answer him. Her one hand is still folding and refolding the pleats. She tries to pull her other hand away from Frank but he holds on to it. "Remember our first meal there? We shared a burger, fries, and a chocolate malt. Only you wouldn't let me have any of the fries."

Stella's hand stops pulling away. "I told you to order your own fries. I like to eat all of them myself."

Frank loosens his grip on the wheel a little. "I still remember the dress you wore that night. Midnight blue."

"I wish I still fit in that dress."

Frank lets go of Stella's hand and taps the side of his head. "You wear it every day up here."

"I thought boys imagined girls naked."

"That too."

They both laugh. Frank loves it when they laugh together. It's almost like they're breathing in sync.

．．．．．

The red neon cyclone circling round a ten-foot ice cream cone glows against the light blue twilight sky. Frank pulls around toward the back of the Whip In and parks near the side door so they're facing the restaurant. Through the windows, Frank can see a few people eating at tables inside. It isn't too busy. Maybe five or six cars in the parking lot.

Neither one of them makes a move to get out of the car and go in. Frank can smell the burgers frying. He's hungry but he doesn't want to move. He likes how being in the car with Stella keeps them in a time capsule together.

Frank points to the poster stuck on the side door. "They still haven't found that Smythe boy."

Stella doesn't say anything.

"It's been almost five months."

"Frank, I need to go."

Frank gets out and hurries around to Stella's side of the car. He opens the door and together they walk into the restaurant. Frank's glad to see there was no one sitting in the back of the restaurant near the restrooms. Sometimes people looking at Stella set her on edge. He follows Stella to the restroom door and watches her go in. He thinks about standing right outside the door but then he hears the lock turn so he walks to the front of the restaurant to order the chocolate malt.

He's pulling two dollars from his wallet to hand to the boy behind the counter when the banging starts. Frank drops the malt and rushes to the back of the restaurant. Stella is inside the restroom banging on the door. The door is still locked. Frank can't get to her.

"Twist the lock, Stell. It's up above the handle."

Stella doesn't say anything. She keeps banging.

Frank runs up to the front. The boy is wiping the counter where the malt had spilled.

"My wife is locked in the bathroom. I need a key."

"Just a minute, mister."

"I don't have a minute. My wife's in there. She could hurt herself."

"Okay. Okay." The boy reaches under the counter and hands a key to Frank.

Frank's hands shake as he puts the key in the lock and turns it. He pushes the door open slowly, carefully, because he can feel Stella's weight against it. Her fists are clenched in tight balls and her forehead is bright red. She must have been banging the door with her fists and her head. Or the wall. Frank doesn't know. He steps toward her and she puts her fists up.

"It's me, Stell. It's your Frankie."

She doesn't move but her eyes look jumpy. Like she's seeing a monster. Frank steps toward her. Closer. Closer. Finally he puts his arms around her. "I got you, sweetheart. You're all right." He raises her chin to look at her face. No cuts. But her forehead is completely red. She might get black eyes this time.

· · · · ·

Frank opens the door of the car and helps her in. The moment he sits down, she leans over and puts her head on his thigh. "No, Stella, you need to sit up and stay awake. I need to make sure you don't have a concussion."

Frank is helping her sit up when the boy from the counter

comes out with a fresh chocolate shake and some ice in a towel. "I'm sorry, mister. Is she going to be all right?"

"Yes. She got a little disoriented. That's all."

The boy nods. He hands Frank the ice and the malt. Frank notices the boy's name stitched on his shirt.

"Thank you, Sam."

Sam smiles. "I'm sorry it happened, sir. My grandpa got that way. We finally had to put him at the Oaks." Then he turns and goes back inside.

Frank holds the malt so Stella can take a few sips. It seems to revive her and she sits up straighter. Frank puts the towel on her forehead.

"Ow! What happened? That hurts, Frankie."

"You tripped, Stella. The floors were wet in there and you tripped. They gave us a free malt."

"Mmmm . . . I love chocolate."

"I know you do, sweetheart. How about sharing a little?"

Frank leans over for a sip but Stella turns her head so Frank can't have any.

She giggles.

Just like that, her confusion is gone and she's with him again.

Frank backs out of their parking spot. Stella holds his hand and sips the malt. Frank hesitates. He can't go to the VFW dance. Someone would notice her forehead. It might start purpling up. He could go back home, but she looks so happy sipping the shake. Truth is, he loves going out with her.

As he turns north out of the Whip In, he sees Enrique standing under the Whip In sign like he's waiting for his son Nando to pick him up. Maybe they worked on different farms today.

The way the red neon light is washing over Enrique, he looks like one of those saints on grocery store candles. Enrique waves and it feels to Frank like he's just been blessed.

"I swear that man can make flowers sprout from rocks," says Frank.

"Remember those herbs he gave us to help me have a baby, Frankie?"

Frank nods. He remembers. Those herbs didn't work but he wonders if Enrique knows an herb that would stop his Stella from losing her mind.

About a mile up the road from the Whip In, the wrought-iron gates of the Oaks Rest Home march along the side of the road. Stella looks at the black vertical lines. "I don't ever want to go there, Frankie."

"I know you don't, Stella."

"But I heard that boy say that's where they put old people like me."

"Don't you worry about what anyone says. I'll take care of you." Frank had always told her he would take care of her. It might be a little harder now. But he can do it. As long as he can drive, he could keep her with him. She loves to go on drives. It relaxes her.

Inside the car, they can stay Frank and Stella. If he turns around and goes back to their regular lives, he'd be an old man with his batty wife. He and Stella are so much more. They're the first couple on the dance floor at homecoming. They're the ones who ran away and got married after graduation. They're never missing a dance at the VFW hall every Friday night. They're six miscarriages until they gave up. They are sixty years of marriage.

If Frank keeps driving, she'll stay with him. He can stop for gas and takeout and never have to be too far away from her. People run away all the time. Maybe that's what happened to the Smythe boy. Tommy.

As if Stella can hear what he's thinking, she says, "Frankie, remember that time we went driving and we tried to get lost? We kept driving and driving trying to end up someplace where we'd never been. Remember that?"

"Except we forgot about getting gas. Remember? We ran out and got stuck."

Stella giggles. "I remember we kissed for a long time in the middle of some field."

Frank remembers.

"Wanna go get lost, Stella?"

"I do, Frankie."

Frank notices the city limits sign flash by their headlights when Stella says those words. Franks takes it as a good sign, like another blessing to begin their adventure.

Frank keeps driving and driving. He stops for gas and coffee. He turns on the radio and changes the station until he finds a song they like. Sometimes, when the radio doesn't pick up a station, he sings to Stella. Elvis songs are her favorite. Frank can sing pretty near every word of "Love Me Tender."

When she falls asleep, Frank worries she'll be disoriented when she wakes up. But she isn't. She's still with him.

"I love you, Frankie."

Frank can hear the smile in her voice. He can't see her face but he imagines her lying in their bed on their wedding night, her chestnut hair all over the white pillow and a dreamy, sleepy smile on her face.

When she falls asleep again, Frank has no idea where they are or how far away they are from where they started. It's pitch-black outside. The moon is past full but it's slipped behind some clouds. He guesses it's two or three in the morning. Maybe later. The roads are starting to curve and it seems like they're driving through some hills, but he isn't sure. At first, not knowing where he is keeps him awake. The wondering excites him. The plan is working. If they stay in the car, Stella won't ever leave him. He'll keep driving and they can slide back and forth across every dance floor they've ever danced on. The Fred High gym at homecoming. The VFW hall every Friday night. Their living room. It won't matter. He'll dance every dance with her. All he has to do is reach across the seat and hold her hand. He can close his eyes and she'll be in his arms. They'll be floating across the dance floor. He'll be leaning in for a kiss. He'll be falling into her.

He'll land in her arms like always.

What if there wasn't a past or a future. What if we don't need to document our history or measure our progress. What if everything exists all at once. I am wondering if it's possible to be aware of everything in one moment. Like we're in the middle of the fireworks display. We're not waiting for the next one or remembering the last one. We simply are in the middle of this display of light. And it is never over.

NANDO

I'M HERE TO PICK UP SOME WORKERS, SHERIFF. NO, sir, I do not know if they are illegal or not. You can ask them. Of course, they probably won't show up while you're here.

One of the vineyard owners called my father last night and said he needs some extra hands. We got the word out pretty late so I'm not sure anyone is going to show up. I'll wait another half hour.

What are you doing?

Are you still looking for him?

Yeah, I knew Tommy. I went to school with him. Also, I work with my father on all the farms around here. We saw him everywhere. Not since last May, though. Wow. Five months already.

My father called him a *brujo*.

It means magician. I think he called him that because of how he'd show up out of the blue. We'd look up from whatever crop we were picking and he'd be standing there. Sometimes he'd be looking at us. Sometimes at the sky or the dirt. Then we'd go back to our work and when we'd look up again, he'd be gone. Like he disappeared.

At first, my father thought he was a bad omen. But I told him he's a kid at my school. A weirdo. An outsider. My father stopped thinking he was a bad omen but he still called him a *brujo*. He said he walked with the spirits. Not like he's dead or anything. More like he has an ability to, I don't know, interact with that world.

That's what my father believes. I don't know if it's true. My father sees things. And then he sees the thing behind the thing. The life force. The energy. In Mexico, they call people like him a *curandero*. Healer. He knows what plants cure headaches and sore joints. He knows what to put on crops to keep grasshoppers away. That's why the farmers around here hire him. Sometimes when he's working a field, he will taste the dirt and know what it needs to make their crops stronger. He's usually right. My father is smart in a different kind of way.

He could charge a lot more money but he says money has no energy. That's how he thinks. He takes money, just enough to live on, but he gets a lot of food as payment. Eggs. Beans. Squash. We always have plenty to eat. When someone slaughters a pig and we've worked their fields, they always give us meat. My father says he'd rather die with a full belly than a full wallet. Me, I want both. I'm starting to manage the money now that I'm older. I'm glad. I charge more. We have a little bit of money now. There are things I want to do. Sometimes when you're Mexican, even if you're born here, people look at you like you can't do anything but manual labor. I love my father but I don't want to work in the fields my whole life.

But you know what? He won't work for anybody. Certain farmers, he won't go on their land. Like that man who got killed in the pull-out. He said no to his lavender fields even though he knew how to cure that mold. He said the man had a shadow around him. He won't work for certain people if he sees that they are *malos*. Bad. I'm glad he says no, that he has a choice. He can't be bought by anyone. I think it's the way my father keeps his dignity. I'm not sure I would be able to do the same thing.

No, he's not a fortune-teller. He doesn't see the future. It's more like he sees an energy. Remember that old couple who drove off the cliff together? I was picking up my father at the Whip In last week. I saw him waving to them. I asked who they were and he called them *los pájaros*. The birds. I asked him what he meant and he shrugged his shoulders. When I heard they went missing and the police later found their bodies at the bottom of a cliff, I showed my father their picture in the newspaper. I asked him if he knew they were going to fly off a cliff and he said no. *Solo vi como los pájaros bonitos*. He only saw them as beautiful birds.

About Tommy? That's all he said: *brujo*. Yeah, he called him that before he went missing. Afterwards, I asked him if he thought Tommy was dead. Like no longer breathing dead. He said what I thought he would say, that ghosts aren't dead. Ghosts are spirit bodies. They're alive to him. He talks to my mother all the time.

Me? I have no idea. I don't see the spirit world the way my father does. To me, Tommy was a *muchacho loco*. On that red bike, wearing those safety goggles from science class. Sometimes he had a girl with him. That gave me hope. If a weirdo like that could get a girl, maybe I could. Someday. My father says it will happen. He says everything takes time. Just like plants growing.

Yeah, I talked to Tommy. Not a lot. Like I said, he was strange. One time, my father and I were out here picking up some extra workers to go out to the Traverses' other farm near Poteet. It was early morning. When? Let's see, I think it was about a week or two before Tommy disappeared. Yeah, that's right, because we were pulling beets and potatoes that day so it would have to be April.

I heard that high-pitched whine of his bike coming up 281. He skidded into the pull-out and started tearing through that trash can. He threw the trash everywhere. You should have seen it. Styrofoam cups. Empty water bottles. Soda cans. Bags of half-eaten food from the Whip In. He went through all of it. Nasty. No one musta emptied that thing for a while.

Then he started searching under the trees and cedars. Only he didn't put the trash back. I went up to him and asked him what he was looking for. He kept saying, "My notebook. Have you seen it? My notebook. Have you seen it?" And the whole time he was digging around in the bushes. Even the cactus. It was a good thing he had those safety goggles on and a long-sleeve shirt, but I am pretty sure he got spines in his hands.

I told him I hadn't seen it and it looked like he was going to have a fit. His eyes were darting around and around. Then he jumped on his bike, peeled out of the pull-out without looking if someone was coming, and left all the trash everywhere. Fucking weirdo.

My father made *me* clean up the pull-out. I was so pissed. The white kid makes the mess and the Mexican cleans it up. But you know what? I kept looking on the side of the road for the notebook. Why? Because he looked so desperate. Like he'd lost the most important thing in the world. You want to help someone like that even if you're pissed at them. I stopped the truck a couple of times because I thought I saw something white in the grass by the road. It wasn't the notebook. Just some pages. It had some writing on it. Stuff about particles and space. I don't know if they were from the notebook. They could have been. I mean, everyone knew he was a freak about science. His notebook could have blown off the back of his bike. Anyway, I picked them up. I was going to give them to him, but he disappeared before I could.

You know what my father said every time I got back in the truck with another scrap of paper? *"Tienes buen corazón."* Me. I have a good heart. Me. I'm pissed at that kid and I'm looking for his stupid notebook. Why should I help him if he can't keep track of his own shit? Or clean up after himself? You know? But my father's right. Even if I don't want to, I help people. If you have a good heart, you know when you're doing the wrong thing. You know it and you can't do it.

Drives me crazy.

That *muchacho loco* is gone and I'm still looking for his notebook.

Maybe time doesn't exist.

We have this clock at home. Dad says it was made in 1898. He winds it on Wednesday and Sunday. If he forgets, it stops. Time doesn't stop. The measuring of it stops. But what is time? Minutes? Days? Weeks? Years? I wonder if time doesn't exist even though we measure it. I wonder if time is an illusion that we agree on.

Except we don't agree. Time doesn't pass at the same rate for all of us. Like time moves more slowly in higher elevations and in space. Time is relative to where you are in space and how fast you are moving. Even the atomic clock combines all the measurements and makes adjustments according to space.

Maybe McCloud's right, maybe when I lose stuff, I go into another dimension where time doesn't exist, so that means I can show up at any time, like at that exact moment when I left my notebook in the chair.

CHRISTMAS ORNAMENTS

AS SOON AS THE CAR SLOWS DOWN, DWIGHT wakes up. The wheels turn and drop into what feels like a rocky field. Dwight grabs his ribs and braces himself against the seat. When the car stops, he sits up carefully and looks out the passenger window. It's dark. All he can see is the black shapes of trees. A few branches hang over the hood of their car. He looks out the other side. They're sitting in an empty parking area on the side of a road.

"Holy crap, Mom, where are we?"

"Texas. We passed Austin about an hour ago. You were sound asleep." She turns off the car. "I'm tired, Dwight. The lines on the road are starting to skip around. I need to close my eyes for a bit."

"What time is it?"

"About four in the morning," says his mother, yawning. "Merry Christmas, sweetheart. We'll stop and get a nice meal somewhere after a while. Okay?"

Dwight is about to say okay but he hears his mom's deep breathing and keeps silent. Texas. They're eight hours away from Doddridge, Arkansas. Dwight leans forward and looks up. Texas stars don't look any different from the Arkansas ones.

He presses his feet into the floorboard, trying to stretch his legs and reposition his body so his ribs don't hurt so much. The more awake he gets, the more they ache. Creaking open the door, he mumbles, "Gotta stand up," in case she hears him. He squeezes outside, careful not to scrape the car door on the branches. He knows no one is around but he doesn't want to leave her alone so he stands a few steps from the car.

Four in the morning. Dwight looks around. It's pitch-black. The moon must have already set. He wonders which direction the sun will rise. Wow, they'd driven all night. He's standing in a whole other state. Dwight has never been out of Arkansas before. He'd never stood up to his father before yesterday. He and his mom had never run away from home before last night. The thing is: all these "never before"s came after the same old thing.

As soon as his father walked into the kitchen and sat down for dinner, he looked at his plate, piled high with beans, picked it up, and said, "What is this shit?"

His mom didn't say anything right away, so Dwight tried to make light of it. "Bean helper."

"Shut up, boy. What is this shit, MayLynn? Where's the meat in my dinner?" He waved the plate in front of her face and dropped it on the table. "Don't I make enough money to have meat in my dinner?" Beans slopped everywhere on the table. Nobody moved. One bean fell off the edge of the plate.

"I'm sorry, Wes. I budgeted as best I could but we had some expenses this week." Her voice was a monotone. She didn't look up. "I'll do better, Wes. I promise."

A fly circled the table. It landed on the light fixture above them. Dwight wondered if it could feel the tension rising. Dwight could. He could almost hear it.

"What were your *expenses*, MayLynn? Huh?"

"We had to have a new spatula. I didn't have enough money to get a pound of hamburger and a new spatula."

"What happened to the old spatula?"

"The old one melted."

"Why'd you cook the spatula, MayLynn?"

His father leaned across the table. Dwight knew his father was about to pounce. The minute he twisted his mother's words so it sounded like she did something intentionally wrong, Dwight knew his father's fist was starting to close. Dwight could feel the pulse in his own fists. They closed around the edge of his chair.

Part of him—it used to be the biggest part of him—wished he could disappear at this moment. He didn't want to see what would happen next. But ever since he started high school, ever since he'd gotten a little bigger, he wished he could stop his father. He wished he could beat his father with his own fists. This part felt larger in him right then.

The fly's wings twitched. Its back legs rubbed together. It looked like it was planning its next move.

"I left it too close to a burner."

"Why'd you do that, MayLynn?"

"It was a mistake."

"Why do you make mistakes, MayLynn?"

This time she didn't answer. She'd admitted her guilt. As soon as she admitted her sin, he was going to punish her. Dwight knew it didn't matter if she followed it up with a dozen "I'm sorry"s, the punishment was coming. Everyone at the table knew it. They were seconds away.

"Answer me, MayLynn."

He could just as easily be repeating Dwight's name. He could be bearing down on Dwight. Dwight could have left the front door open too long. Or let the back screen door slam. Or not cleaned the bathroom perfectly. Dwight wondered if his mother ever felt relieved when his father was going after him and not her. He hated feeling that sliver of relief.

"Are you stupid, MayLynn?"

Dwight glanced over at his mother. Her face had no fight in it. Whatever was going to happen, she was going to sit there and take it. How could she do it? Again? Dwight felt anger flare behind his eyes. He could almost hear it pulse in his ears.

"Huh? Stupid? Huh?"

The fly took off.

Dwight stood up. He was almost as tall as his father. "Don't hit her."

His father's head pivoted to Dwight. He forced himself to stand there and straighten up a little taller to meet his father's eyes. At the same time, he felt like he might fall down. He kept staring into his father's black eyes. They were so deep set and heavy lidded that the pupils covered any color. It made him look meaner.

"What's that, boy? You got something to say to me? You're going to take up for your mama?"

"Go to your room, Dwight." The sound of his mother's voice sounded like a march. Usually he obeyed her. Usually, he was glad to leave. But tonight, something was different. Tonight, he wanted to fight back.

"Come on, boy, take your best shot."

Dwight saw the fly light on his father's shoulder. Flies are easy to kill. All he has to do is whack them once. How hard would he have to hit his father to make him stop? He curled his fist into a ball.

"Come on, wuzzy boy. Let me have it."

Dwight's fist rocketed up, but as soon as it left his side, his father grabbed it and twisted his whole arm around his back. It felt like his arm was going to be torn off. Then his father threw him against the wall.

Even though his head bashed against the wall, he was glad to be sliding down it away from his father. For a moment, he liked how the wall felt solid, how it held him. But in the very next minute, he was pinned against it as his father's foot slammed into his back. Once. Twice.

Before the third kick, Dwight felt warm beans splatter everywhere around him. His mother was screaming. "Stop it!" Then he heard her yell, "It's Christmas, Wes. I thought a few presents were more important than your goddamn meat."

Dwight looked up to see the cast-iron skillet in her hand. She must have hit his father once because he was holding the side of his head. She was reeling back to land a second blow but his father was quicker. His fists went into her stomach, her face. She fell back onto the table. The skillet clanked onto the floor.

Dwight tried to get up but pain shot across his back. He tried to slide himself toward his mother but it hurt. He looked up at her on the table. Her head was rolled so she faced him. Her nose was bleeding. Her eye had a cut above it and was swelling already. Still, Dwight could see that she was looking at him, willing him not to move. He knew she was right. He stayed put. If they stopped, he would stop. Eventually.

Only not before he flipped the table so she fell on the floor. Not before he kicked her again and again. Not before he yelled and cussed and kicked Dwight in the stomach one more time for good measure on his way out the back door, into the night, into a bar, into a haze where Dwight knew he would forget his wife and his son lying on the kitchen floor broken, with beans everywhere.

Dwight tried to sit up. The last kick to the stomach had knocked the wind out of him. "Mom?" She wasn't moving. "Mom!" Dwight scooted through the beans and dishes and glasses, toward her. He pulled himself up on an overturned chair. His back and stomach hurt like shit but he pushed himself to get over to her. He rolled her over. Her lip was bleeding. A lot. There were cuts on her face. Maybe she'd been knocked out when she fell on the floor.

She opened her eyes. "Izzhe gone?"

The way she mumbled the question, Dwight wondered if any of her teeth were broken. He nodded. "Yes."

"Are you okay?"

Dwight sat on the floor and leaned against the counter. "Yeah."

He felt his ribs. Even if they were broken, all he could do is tape them. His mother sat up and turned away from Dwight. He could tell she was touching her face, probably checking to see how bad the cuts were.

"Go take a shower, Dwight. I'll clean up in here." She still didn't look at him.

"It's okay. I'll help."

"I don't want your help, Dwight. Please. Go take a shower."

Dwight knew she didn't want him to see her face. He stood up slowly, still leaning on the counter. "Okay," he said, and started to walk away. When he reached the doorway, he stopped. "Mom, I'll be ready next time. I can fight him now." Then he walked to the bathroom and turned on the shower.

Dwight tossed his bean-smeared clothes into the hamper and stepped into the shower. He flinched as the hot water hit the sore places on his back. Then he turned and let the water run over what was already a large red circle on his stomach. At first, the heat felt tender on his skin. Slowly, it helped him relax so that he could breathe into the pain, stretch his diaphragm. He felt his ribs. No, he didn't think anything was broken. Just bruised. Really badly bruised.

Dwight stood with his head directly under the showerhead and didn't move. All the images from the kitchen rushed through his mind, froze him in the hot shower. First the loud tension building to the first punch, then the silence except for the hitting. For his entire life, Dwight had been trapped inside the silence. It didn't matter how hard Dwight tried to be good, it always turned out he was pestering his father and got whacked on the head. If Dwight lied or didn't put something back in the garage that he borrowed, his father took the belt to him. If his mother tried to stop the punishment, then it was worse for both of them. Tonight, though, something besides fear coursed through him. He could feel anger vibrating in his blood. A guttural roar erupted inside him. He tightened his fists so hard they shook. He couldn't stop imagining pummeling his father until he crumpled, until he felt the same fear that Dwight had felt all his life.

Dwight stood in the shower until the water ran cold. When he stepped out, he knew he hated his father. He didn't know what he was going to do about it, but his fear had turned to white-hot rage.

. . . . .

Dwight stood in the doorway of the kitchen. It looked pristine. As if no fight had ever taken place. All the dishes were washed. The floor was mopped. His mother stood at the sink. Her profile was to him and her hair hung down.

"The shower's yours, Mom. You'll need to wait a little for hot water. I kinda stood in there awhile."

She nodded. "Sure."

Dwight noticed that she was holding a dish towel to her mouth. "You okay?"

She nodded, still not looking at him. "Yeah."

"You sure?" He started to walk toward her.

"No, Dwight. Stop!" She turned her back to him. "I'm fine. I'll be fine."

She didn't sound fine. She sounded like her lips were swollen or her teeth were broken. Still, Dwight stopped. He turned to go to his room. "Mom, if we don't kill him, he's going to kill us."

. . . . .

When Dwight walked into the living room in the morning, his father wasn't snoring on the couch. Dwight checked to see if his truck was outside. It wasn't. He crept down the hall to his mother's room. The door was open. No one was there. The bathroom was empty. Dwight crept around the house wondering when his father would get home. Every step reminded him of the fight last night. His back and stomach ached. It was hard to breathe. Still, the anxiety of not knowing where his father was or when he would come home made it harder to breathe. He wished he knew where his mother was. Maybe grocery shopping. Usually she made a really good dinner for Christmas Eve.

Five times over the course of the day, Dwight did that same circuit. Even after his mother came home and started cooking, he kept checking the living room to see if his father was asleep on the couch. He couldn't believe he wanted his father there, snoring or moving slowly and quietly because his head hurt. Usually, Dwight wanted him gone. But now, not knowing when his father would come through the door, Dwight wanted life to go back to what passed as normal. Dwight's stomach churned. His ribs and back ached.

At eight o'clock, he finally sat down in the living room and opened up an ancient issue of *Boy's Life* magazine. He flipped back and forth through it. He'd read it dozens of times. He checked the clock every other second. He watched his mother fill a pot with water and set it on the stove. He felt crazy fidgety.

Where was he? He always came back after the fights. No matter how bad they were. The next day, the house was quieter. All three of them were quieter so as not to wake the argument that still lurked in the corners. Still, he always came home. Until today.

Bang!

Dwight jumped. Was that his father's truck? He looked out the window. No truck lights.

He looked past the undecorated, unlighted Christmas tree, toward the kitchen. His mother's back was to him but he could tell by the way her elbows were crooked that she'd slammed the pot down on purpose. She was gripping it tight in both hands. The harder she held it, the easier she could hold back tears. He'd seen her do it a zillion times. First her eyes would brim up. Then she'd grab on to something. Then her lips would purse together tight till they turned white. She'd exhale and the tears would be gone. All that would be left was blotchy red marks on her cheeks where the hot tears had pooled up under her skin.

Dwight glanced over at the clock. The minute number flopped from three to four. It was 8:04. It felt like an hour had gone by. Dwight looked from the tree to his mom. He wanted to do something. Tonight was the night they decorated the Christmas tree. Always.

"Mom . . ."

She turned. Her split lip was swollen. She had it slathered

with cream so it wouldn't break open and bleed. The red mark on her cheek had lessened but her eye was starting to purple. Her hands hung at her side. She looked at Dwight straight on.

Dwight wanted to turn away, not because of the cuts and bruises. It was the way she stared at him. Like she had nothing on. Like she was completely naked and couldn't cover up. Dwight folded and unfolded the *Boy's Life* magazine in his lap.

"Maybe we could put the lights on the tree." He started to reach for them so he wouldn't have to look at her.

"Don't touch those lights, Dwight."

He stopped and looked at her. Her tone was even. Almost strong. It surprised him.

"Dwight, I want you to go to your room and pack an overnight bag. Don't forget your toothbrush."

The way she said the words pushed Dwight out of the living room. He grabbed a shirt, two pairs of underwear, and a pair of pants. He stuffed them into his school backpack, which was empty of books for the holiday. Then he went to the bathroom and grabbed his toothbrush and the tube of toothpaste. When he came back to the living room, his mother stood by the front door. A small square white suitcase was next to her feet. She looked around the room.

"Is there anything here you can't live without?"

Dwight wasn't sure if she was asking him the question or herself. Dwight looked at the room. His eyes fell on the old *Boy's Life* magazine that he'd read over and over. His mother said she bought it for him but Dwight knew it was the same one he'd read at the hospital that time she had to get stitches in her hand. He knew that she took it for him when she went back to have the stitches out. He almost grabbed it but he reached for the box of twelve Christmas ornaments tucked under the tree instead.

"Why do you want those—?" his mom started to ask, but she stopped.

Then they ran.

A minute before, they were waiting for his father to get home. Now they were running, so fast it was like all their cuts and bruises had healed. The urgency of leaving before he drove up was upon them. They ran toward the old blue Impala parked by the woodshed. They didn't bother opening the trunk. His mom tossed her suitcase in the backseat. Dwight stuffed the backpack by his feet and kept the ornaments on his lap. She fumbled with the keys. Dwight wondered if it had gas. One of the arguments was how there was never enough money for gas or meat or extras. There was never any money.

"I gassed it up earlier today," she said, as if she heard his thought. She turned the key and the engine chugged to life. Dwight looked out to the road. He couldn't see any headlights coming.

She shifted the car into gear and stepped on the gas, pulling out of their driveway and onto the road. Dwight felt the acceleration pin his spine against the seat. It felt good on his ribs. For the first time all day, he could breathe. She kept pressing the gas pedal and Dwight shifted in his seat, leaning forward as if he were riding a horse, urging it onward. He looked behind. Still no lights. Up ahead, the road had one set of headlights coming at them. It could be him. Dwight glanced at his mom. She gripped the steering wheel and looked straight ahead. It reminded Dwight of how he would look straight ahead at the dining room table, trying to be invisible when their arguments started. Dwight ducked his head under the dashboard. As the headlights drew closer, Dwight whispered, "Pass, pass, pass."

It passed.

Dwight turned and looked out the back window, praying that he wouldn't see the brake lights flare and stop in the night. They didn't. He watched them get smaller and smaller. While he was turned around, another car passed them and Dwight watched its two red lights join the smaller red dots farther away. They reminded Dwight of the connect-the-dot game on the backs of cereal boxes where an animal would appear out of seemingly random numbered dots. With each car that passed them, Dwight prayed that none of them would become the animal that would chase after them.

They drove like that for three hours, maybe more. Dwight looking backward. His Mom looking forward. Finally, she pulled into a gas station.

"I have to get more gas and this might be the last one that's open on Christmas Eve. Do you want anything?"

"What do you mean?"

"Do you want a Dr Pepper or some chips?"

Dwight stared at his mother. She had never offered to buy him a Dr Pepper. Ever. He'd asked plenty. But there was never enough money. "Sure."

"Great. Would you pump the gas? I'll go pay and use the restroom."

Dwight nodded and got out. His mom shoved a baseball cap on her head and pulled it down really far so the bruises on her face weren't quite as visible. He watched her walk into the convenience store and listened to the gas gush into the tank. The numbers whirled by on the pump. When it clicked off, the amount was $54.82. More than some of their grocery bills.

As he walked into the store, he saw his mom handing the clerk a hundred-dollar bill. He stopped and stared. She glanced at him. "The restroom is back in the corner. See you in the car?"

Dwight opened the door to the bathroom. It was cold in there. Like a refrigerator. He had to concentrate on letting go and peeing. It took a while. He kept wanting to think about the hundred-dollar bill. He wondered where she got it.

When he got back in the car, his mom handed him the Dr Pepper and a large opened bag of chips. She clinked her Coke bottle with his. Dwight did not clink back.

"Merry Christmas, Dwight."

Dwight held the cold glass bottle in his hand. He could hear the carbonation bubbles fizz and pop. The cherry and cola smells made his mouth water. "Mom, where'd you get the money?"

She turned the car on and pulled out of the gas station. "Don't worry. I didn't steal it."

Dwight took a sip. The soda tickled his tongue. He was thinking about all the arguments. All the bruises. All the stitches.

"But, Mom, I thought we didn't have any money. I thought . . ."

"I know. Money was always the argument. So how do I have money?"

"Yeah."

"I put a dollar aside the first time he hit me. That was before you were born. I told myself if he didn't hit me for a whole year, I'd put it back in with the grocery money. I set aside ten dollars that first year."

Dwight listened to the tires carry them down the highway. He wondered if they would be running away if she'd spent the money on meat last night.

"But, Mom . . ." Dwight tried to figure out what to ask. "How much . . . ?"

"I withdrew a couple thousand dollars from the bank today."

"Holy shit." He did the math in his head. They got married a year before he was born. He was fourteen, almost fifteen. If they had a fight every month, it still didn't add up. "But that's barely two hundred dollars."

"I counted every bruise, every stitch, every broken plate and glass. When he beat you, I charged him double."

"How'd you hide it?"

"Under your mattress for a while. Then I put it in a bank under your name. I'd always go make a deposit on Saturday morning."

Dwight knew that's when his father was usually asleep on the couch. "Why didn't you leave?"

"Sometimes he was nice. Sometimes he was sorry. When you were real little, he laid off me. When it started back up, I made a plan."

"But, Mom, if you'd done what he wanted, if you'd bought the meat, maybe it wouldn't have happened." Dwight thought about their house. He never invited friends over because he never had any toys or games or balls. Every Christmas, he'd asked for a bike until he gave up last year. Every scrap of furniture, every book, every little everything was second- or third-hand. He'd thought his mom was scrimping and saving and trying to make his father's paychecks last. He'd thought she was doing the best she could. Dwight touched his ribs. She might as well have kicked him, too.

He heard the blinker clicking and realized his mom was pulling off the highway. It was pitch-black except for their headlights. They must be in the middle of nowhere. She pulled the car onto the gravel shoulder and stopped, turning off the car and snapping off the lights. Dwight could hardly see her profile.

"Dwight, do you really think it's about money?"

"Yeah. I mean, that's what he always got so mad about."

Dwight heard her take a deep breath. "If you think we should go back, I will. But let me ask you this. When he hit you last night, did he do it because you did something wrong? Or did he do it because he liked hitting you?"

Already the car was chilling down. It was cold outside. Dwight shivered. He thought back to his father's face last night. When he grabbed Dwight's fist and twisted his arm, he looked pissed. When he was questioning his mother about the spatula, he looked mean and upset. When he held the plate of beans in front of her face, he looked— Wait. He was smiling. He knew what was going to happen. He made it happen. He wanted it.

"Let's keep going, Mom."

. . . . .

Now she's asleep and he's standing in an empty parking lot waiting for the sun to rise on Christmas morning. He'd left her gift under his bed. He should have grabbed it instead of the ornaments. It was stupid to take them. So what if they were the last breakable things in the house? Each year when he put them on the tree, Dwight watched over them, protected them, kept them from getting broken. He liked how they made their living room look less secondhand for the time they were up. When he took them off the tree unbroken, he felt proud. Like he'd saved the world from ending.

Dwight opens the car door so slowly it doesn't make a sound. He reaches inside and grabs the box of ornaments. Carefully, he climbs up on the hood. One by one, he hangs the silver globes on the cedar branches above his head. It feels good to stretch his arms and ribs a little. Just as he is about to hang the last one, he sees a pair of clear plastic goggles wrapped around one of the branches. They look like the kind he uses in science classes. It's strange to think about school on Christmas morning. Then Dwight realizes he won't be going back to his old school. Ever. He doesn't know where he's going next. Maybe wherever it is, he'll have friends he can invite over to his house. Maybe it will be a place friends want to hang out.

He pulls the goggles off the branch, puts them on, and tries to see himself in the side-view mirror but it's still too dark. He probably looks like a science nerd. That's cool. He likes science. Maybe he'll use them at his next school. Maybe he'll wear them a lot to look weird. Sometimes it's cool to look weird.

Dwight squeezes back into the passenger seat. His mother barely moves. He looks up at the ornaments. At first, all he can see are round shapes in the trees. As the sky lightens, the ornaments turn gray, then silver. When the sun rises, they change from purple to rose to orange. They're turning gold when he hears his mother yawn and sit up. Dwight slides the goggles up on his forehead and smiles.

"Merry Christmas, Mom."

Hawking said that if the rate of the universe's expansion one second (was there time back then?) after the big bang had been smaller by even one part of a hundred thousand million million, then the universe would have collapsed and no intelligent life could have evolved.

That's pretty specific. No wonder people want to think there was a supreme being. Did a god or a supreme being know that one exact moment? Did it create the so-called big bang? Is there a greater intelligence out there? There is no evidence for it. There is evidence for a striving toward life. If something is created, its impulse is to live. But is that God? Or energy?

I don't think there is this supreme being who thought up the universe and began putting it together day by day. I don't believe that. I think the Bible is a big storybook that is trying to explain how we got here. That's what all stories try to do: try to explain our reason for being.

Isn't that why I'm writing in this journal?

The big bang seems more real to me than a supreme being. Look at how astronomers have proved that space is expanding. They proved that. So if you rewind the tape thirteen billion years, then why not start with a hot dense state that leads to the big bang that leads to galaxies and stars, which are still expanding?

It's like when one exact sperm from whoever my dad was connected with the one exact egg from whoever my mom was, my cells started dividing. A different sperm with a different egg on a different month and I would not be writing this sentence.

I don't think a supreme being had anything to do with it.

HALLIE

FOR CRYING OUT LOUD, EUGENE CALDWELL, I HAVE known you since you were a spit of a thing. Don't give me any of that "Ms. Stillwell, I need to ask you a few questions" baloney. Knock on my door, say, "Hello, Hallie," like you would any other day of the week. If you get all official on me, I'll official you right off my property.

That's better. Have a seat.

Yes, it is pleasant up here on the porch. Yes, the weather is mighty fine for January. Eugene, I'm eighty-four years old. Please don't waste my time with pleasantries.

So what is it this time? Do you need to organize another search across the property? How many have we had? That first week, you pretty near combed every inch of the ranch. After that, it seems like we had a search every other week until well after school let out. I've lost count of how many times you've run dogs across the property looking for Tommy. My goats have done more running than grazing this year.

I know people are upset about the pull-out. What am I supposed to do about that? It's a patch of dirt, for crying out loud. It was there when my granddaddy started ranching here. Hell, maybe that little ledge of land was beachfront a million years ago and dinosaurs stopped there like people do now.

We've had more than a few dramas at the pull-out over the years. Back when my daddy was alive, I remember the Texas Rangers combing the area looking for a girl and a boy. They'd run away to get married. I was a teenager. I remember thinking it was highly romantic. Only it ended in tragedy. The girl's father found them in that outbuilding five hundred yards from the pull-out and shot them both. Should have shot himself too while he was at it. He went crazy. Hid in the back of what became Clark's Salvage Yard until Sheriff Hamilton hauled him in. Yeah, that was well before your time.

You know what my daddy did after that murder? The ranch hands circled the property on horseback at night. Eighteen hundred acres. After two horses pulled up lame, he stopped that public service. I guess they came across a few illegals, but that was pretty normal. After a while, it didn't make much sense to him. Anybody who stopped at that pull-out had a damn good reason: rest, lost, or broke down. Daddy had a ranch to run. He couldn't be policing a dirt patch by the side of the road.

You can do what you want with that pull-out. Pave it over. Fence it off. I don't care. But that's not why you came out here to see me, is it, Sheriff Caldwell?

What do I think about particle physics? You're kidding me, right? Yes, I've heard the talk. Tommy was very fascinated with all scientific phenomenon. I used to watch him out there, wandering around looking at flies on manure. He was a strange kid. So what? All kids are strange. You used to have quite a fascination with making fireworks as I recall, Eugene.

Do I think he's gone into another dimension? Hell no. Now look here, Eugene. What's going on is totally normal. A kid goes missing. The whole town is up in arms. Every day that goes by is worse. Of course they want to believe some extraterrestrial, time travel theory. They haven't even found one shoe that belongs to Tommy.

Eugene, I've lived on this ranch my entire life. I am not a stranger to death. Between Mexicans crossing over, dying of thirst, and animals getting tore up by coyotes, I have seen my share of dead bodies. Now I know we haven't found a body, so there's still hope, but I wouldn't blame you if you stopped actively looking for Tommy Smythe.

Isn't that what you are here to tell me?

I understand. It's been almost a year and there's no sign of the boy. You can't spend any more man-hours on it. Yes, I know the Smythes are going to be upset and I know that Simmons woman is saying if the pull-out hadn't been there, that girl wouldn't have murdered her husband. She might persuade the Smythes that the pull-out was the reason Tommy went missing. I know what people are saying. You'd be amazed at how news travels out here. Are you here to warn me that there might be some sort of backlash when you tell them you aren't making Tommy your top priority every waking minute?

I know you want to find him. We all do. I thought pursuing

that adoption angle was your best hope. Kids are curious about that sort of thing.

If he was picked up by a stranger, well, there's no way to know what happened with that. You've still got his picture out there, right?

No, I don't think he just ran away. Kids leave clues.

Hell, Eugene, Mexicans are better prepared to cross the border than Tommy and they still die. There are some sad cases out here. I hate it when I find a pair of shoes in one of the goat paths. I know someone put them there, right at the end, so I'd find a body. And I always do.

You know I've also heard that Simmons girl is wanting to put together a memorial for Tommy. I don't think that's a bad idea. You might want to put your efforts toward that. It'll help people move on. And body or not, we need to move on.

I appreciate the heads-up. I really do. I doubt they'll bother me. Most people don't take the time to come all the way up here, and when they do, they usually find I'm pretty hospitable. Sometimes I invite them to live here.

That ruffled a few feathers, didn't it? Yes, she's still living with me. We get on pretty good. She's a good girl. She's learning English. She's helping me with everything from groceries to writing checks to paying the workers. I'm thinking about ruffling every feather in the county and leaving the entire Stillwell Ranch to her. You heard right. Who else should I give it to? You know my only child's dead.

Who cares if she can't hang on to it? It's just dirt. If it belongs to anyone, it belongs to the animals. They use it more than I do. Look out there. This land has been in my family for three generations. We've paid taxes on it. We've worked it. It's given us a good life. Before us, it belonged to the Mexicans, the Spanish, the French. At one time, we would have been the illegals. It's land. People put borders on it and make laws around it. But I don't really own it. I just walk on it. All I am is one person standing between earth and sky. If you start looking at the land that way, all the laws and boundaries around ownership seem silly.

That's probably why I let Tommy wander around here. Why I didn't throw him off. He seemed to appreciate the notion of standing on some dirt between heaven and earth.

I keep thinking he's going to find his way back if he isn't dead. People are mostly law abiding. You have some bad ones, but really, I think people tend to choose kindness over cruelty. That golden rule? Treat people like you like to be treated. It's in our DNA.

Yes, Eugene, things get a little odd from time to time. That girl with the pickax, for one. But I bet at one time she was a sweet little girl who played with dolls. Something happened to her that twisted her up inside. She wasn't always like that, I guaran-damn-tee you.

What would have happened if I'd turned Maricela away when she came wandering up here with that boy on her hip? How do you think that little boy would do if she were desperate and scared and hungry? You never know how you are going to touch some people. I think people are basically good. Really good. That golden rule has been working on us for centuries.

People think this world is much crueler and more brutal

now. But it's not. We only hear about it faster. People have those little computer phones in their pockets and they hear about disasters and meannesses at the speed of light. They think things are worse. But I don't. You go stand on some dirt between heaven and earth and see for yourself. Life is pretty fine.

I think, wherever Tommy is, he knows it.

Rachel says I'm supposed to pay more attention to the way people feel. I can't. Feelings are too mysterious. They take too much time to observe and then it's usually wrong. She says I should start by observing my own feelings. That's even harder. As soon as I observe one feeling, it's gone.

I need to tell her that some people have found that you can't describe feelings because of what's known as the specious present. As soon as you observe the exact moment you are in, it is gone.

CHUY

EXCUSE ME, SIR. IS THIS WHERE THE TRUCKS PICK up workers?

I've been working on a farm nearby. The Traverses' place. You know them?

Yes, they have a lot of work, a lot of planting. I could stay on but I made a promise to someone I'd keep going north.

You need some help? With the shovel, I mean. You want me to dig something while I'm waiting?

Sure. Where do you want it? Here? Okay. One post hole coming up.

Thank you. Consuelo made me speak English all the time. Even watching television. No telenovelas. If a show came on with Spanish subtitles, she'd tape paper in front of them. You know how I learned the most English? Comic books. I love them. I read as many as I could. Superman. Batman. The Avengers. Consuelo didn't mind. As long as they were in English. She said

I had to dream in English. I guess it worked, but I can't tell if I dream in English or Spanish. They both sound normal to me.

You could call Consuelo my mother. She raised me.

My parents live in Mexico. They never got papers. We lived across the river from the American colonias. I went back and forth all the time when I was little. After a while I stayed with Consuelo. My parents wanted me to learn English and have a better life, so I stayed and went to school on the American side. I never got papers either, but everyone thought I was Consuelo's boy. The people who knew didn't care. Consuelo had papers and her three daughters were born here. She was glad to have a boy. One more mouth to feed is hard, but one more mouth also means two more hands to work. As soon as I could hold a shovel, I went out to work. But only after school.

Consuelo made sure school was first. She made me pronounce every word right. No *share* for chair. She is *bien mandona*. Very bossy. She's the reason I'm headed north. She made me promise I'd leave as soon as I graduated high school. She says living down there is like dying and if I don't leave, she'd kill me. She might. She carries a knife at her waist.

The colonias. You ever been to the border? No, they're not even towns. And the houses aren't really houses. It's a hard place. It's kind of nowhere. You're not in Mexico and you're not in America. Well, you are but you're not. Consuelo ended up in the colonias because she didn't have much money after her husband left and never came back.

I told her I would send her money when I was working but she said not to. She says it takes five minutes to get used to something better but it takes a whole lifetime to get used to ugliness. She says she's used to the ugliness now. It's a hard place.

No, she never adopted me. My parents tried to come back across the border several times but they got stopped. Finally, they stayed in Mexico. For a while I sneaked across to see them. But then one day I stopped. When you're young, immigration doesn't see you. But as soon as you start to look like a worker, they hassle you. And if you don't speak English, they really hassle you. I haven't seen my parents since I was ten.

I have papers but they're fake. Consuelo paid a lot of money to get them. That's why I am walking and sleeping in fields. She told me to get very far away from the border before I use them and start acting like an American. She said the farther I get from the border, the less people will know what official papers look like. I know it will be hard, but I think I can make it. Consuelo told me wherever I end up, I should go to school. She said immigration wouldn't look for me there. I don't know. She might be right.

Consuelo will tell my parents I went north. They will be happy. I know they want me to have a good life. It seems like my parents gave me up, but that's not true. When you're on the bottom and you're sinking in the mud, you push your children up and hope someone will catch them. Even if it means you drown.

Is this deep enough?

Oh wait. You need some help carrying that?

That's a beautiful cross, sir. I like the way the wood is curved on the corners and the bronze is set into the middle. It looks strong. It looks like your love for that person is strong. Someone is lucky to be remembered with this cross.

Your son? Oh, señor, I'm sorry.

Here, let me help you. Hold it straight. I'll pack in the dirt. My name is Chuy, by the way. Jesus. But everyone calls me Chuy.

Nice to meet you, Mr. Smythe.

When did he die?

He disappeared? That means he could come back. People can disappear like ghosts and they come back. It happens all the time on the border. You never know. Some people get picked up by Immigration and get sent back to Mexico. Some people go north. And then they come back.

What's his name? Tommy? In the colonias, if you never find the body, you always have hope. They can come back. People disappear. Parents. Sisters. Even the drunk old men. They come back. Sometimes with a lot of money. Sometimes beat up. If they don't come back, you never know. They could be in Hollywood. They could be rich. You never know. Tommy could come back.

A year is a long time. But it could happen.

It took me six months to walk here from the colonias. I took my time. I worked on the way, but walking is like digging a big hole with a shovel. It takes time, but you get there.

You want me to get some rocks to put around the base? Don't worry. I don't mind. This land has a lot of rocks.

I wonder if that truck is coming. I probably got here too late. Mr. Travers said I could get more work around here. He also said the woman who owns that land out there always needs help with her goats and sheep. He says she takes in boarders like me. Has a girl and her son living there now. I could walk up there. If the truck doesn't come, maybe I will.

Yeah, I slept out there last night. Did you know there was an old stone house straight out that way? It's falling down but I slept there. No, I never make fires. It's too dangerous.

No, I'm not scared. I mean, I keep to myself. I watch out. I learned a lot listening to people who crossed over. If you are traveling alone, you look for a place to sleep while you are walking. Under a tree is good. Or sometimes you pass by a ledge with flat ground underneath. Somehow you have to mark the place in your mind. But you keep walking. Then when the sun is setting, you stop and you wait. When it's dark, you go back to that place you found. You need to go back to it in the dark because you don't want anyone to see you. If someone sees you go back to the place, they could rob you when you are asleep. Or worse.

I've walked a mile, or more, back to a place. Sometimes, if I don't see a place during the day, I walk a long time after it's dark and then I lie down and hope for the best. Once you lie down, you listen. You listen for any sounds. You learn the difference between a man and an armadillo. They are difficult to tell apart. The armadillos are so loud they sound like men stumbling around.

Gradually, I stop listening for the sounds and I breathe. After a while, it's like I become the air. I start to disappear into the night. Then I fall asleep.

Sometimes strange sounds wake me up and I see people,

sometimes three or four, walking through the field. They look like ghosts. You can't see their legs. Just the shapes of their bodies moving over a field. That's another way to travel. At night. I couldn't do it. It's too hard to find a safe place to sleep during the day. Plus I would be too nervous to fall asleep. Someone could walk up on me. At least, at night, it's easier to hide in the shadows.

Is that enough rocks? I think we need two more.

Yes, I see a lot of things at night. Sometimes I think that all the people sleeping in their beds have no idea of the life going on around them. There is a whole highway of people, traveling in the night, out in their fields, crossing their roads. We are invisible to them.

Sometimes, there are people out there who are invisible even when we see them.

Well, it's a strange story. You probably won't believe me. Not too long ago, maybe a month, I was south and west of here. I'd just left a farm that had me digging postholes for a new fence. I probably dug five hundred holes. This one was easy, señor.

Anyway, I found a really good place to sleep. There was a tree up above and a deep hole under a ledge. It looked like animals had dug it out or the wind had eroded it. After I got in there, a storm started. I could hear the thunder. The lightning was flashing all around. One time it flashed, I swear I saw a person. About as close as that trash can. The thunder and lightning were right on top of each other. No rain yet. The whole field was filled with electricity and noise. I kept watching that person. I was worried he would get hit by lightning. I yelled at him to come over where I was. He heard me because he looked at me. I swear he looked at me because it was very, very bright. I could see his face. There was lightning everywhere and then he disappeared. I'm not kidding. I ran over there because I thought maybe he was struck by lightning and fell down. But he was gone. I'm telling you it was like he stepped into a closet and disappeared. I swear. I know it sounds crazy. But there wasn't any trace of him. Anywhere. Nothing. I was scared to keep standing there. Maybe there was an entrance to another world and, if I stepped the wrong way, I wouldn't come back. Then the rain poured down and I ran to my hole. When I looked back, it was raining so hard I couldn't see a thing. It was like a curtain of water.

Now I'm not sure I saw anything. Maybe it was a trick with the lightning. But maybe it was a spirit or an alien. You know, an extraterrestrial.

Like I said, sometimes I woke up in the middle of the night and people were walking through the fields. At least I thought they were people. Maybe they weren't. What if I was seeing aliens? What if I was seeing into another universe? It could be, right? You probably think I am crazy. Or that I read too many comic books. Comic books always have aliens. And heroes jumping across space and time to save the day.

Consuelo says spirits walk the earth. She believes there is a time, right after someone dies, when you can see him. Like they haven't crossed over. She says you can talk to them and they can hear you. She talks to her spirits all the time. She says they talk to her but I'm not so sure of that. Because they only talk to her when she wants to make me do something I don't want to do. "I can hear your *abuelo* Juan Pedro telling me you need to take chemistry so you can be a doctor." Or something like that.

There. The cross is strong. You know, you could leave a message for your son here. On the cross. In case he comes back, so he knows you are still looking for him. People will talk about this cross, I think. They will know about your son. I know about your son. I will look for him.

Every night, when I go to sleep outside, I pray that I will wake up in the morning. I pray I will be safe. I never know when I go to sleep if something might happen. Anything could. Poisonous spiders. Robbers. Mountain lions. You don't know.

When I wake up, I'm glad to be alive. I'm glad to stand up and keep walking. But you know what? I'm still uncertain. Any minute something can change. A storm. A snake. I thought I would feel safe in the morning. But I don't.

What I'm trying to say is, it's hard to live with not knowing. Like you want to know if your son is dead or alive. But it's uncertain. This life is a mystery.

We have to live each day with the mystery.

ACKNOWLEDGMENTS

In a very real way, this debut novel is in your hands because a whole lot of people said, "Yes. Keep going. You can do it. Wow. Love it." Bear with me while I try to acknowledge all of them here.

I began this novel while I was an M.F.A. student at that holy place on the hill in Montpelier called Vermont College of Fine Arts. Every lecture and workshop shaped me as a writer, and I am down on my knees grateful for advisors Sarah Ellis, Jane Kurtz, Sharon Darrow, and Julie Larios for their wisdom and coaching and patience. A special kekekekekek goes out to my class of Thunderbadgers.

After I graduated from VCFA, I was lucky enough to fall into the finest clutch of critique mates ever: Anne Bustard, Bethany Hegedus, and Liz Garton Scanlon. Writing is a less lonely business with you ducks quacking along with me.

This novel has grown in size and depth as the result of these readers: Kimberly Garcia, Jim Phillips, Greg Delaney, John Thomas Harms, Brian Yansky, Cynthia Leitich Smith, Meredith

Davis, and Rod and Isabella Russell-Ides, as well as the Palacios retreat group: Kathi Appelt, Rebecca Kai Dotlich, and Jeanette Ingold. Thank you for every minute of your time and attention.

A writer needs a cache of people she can call with the odd question. Thankfully, all these folks were willing to answer my calls and e-mails: Chris Bratton, Rod Davis, Tomas Salas, Susanna Sharpe, Brian Anderson, Tim Crow, Cassandra Ricks, Carol Ann Sayle and Larry Butler, John and Medora Barkley, Paul MacNamara at Central Machine Works, Libbey Aly at the Blanco Chamber of Commerce, and Beth Boggess at the National Center of Farmworker Health.

I am the luckiest person to have the biggest support system of nears and dears in the world: that means you. Every conversation has mattered.

Two sections in this novel require specific thank-yous:

In 1997, journalist Denise Gamino wrote a compelling *Austin American-Statesman* article about Lela and Raymond Howard, who wandered away from their home in Salado. Her reporting inspired "The Last Dance."

A huge debt of gratitude goes to *Austin Chronicle* editor Louis Black, who believed in me as a writer and sent me to interview Karla Faye Tucker at the Gatesville Prison with the amazing documentary photographer Alan Pogue. "Lost" is the result of his faith.

I also want to express my deep appreciation to Erin Murphy and the community that is EMLA as well as to Joy Peskin, Simon Boughton, Angus Killick, Elizabeth H. Clark, and all the Macmillan folks in the Flatiron Building. Thank you for saying yes.

And finally, to Jeanne and Ed Daniels, none of the above would have been possible without your support and love. Angels, you are.